SHATNER QUEST

JEFF BURK

Eraserhead Press
Portland, OR

ERASERHEAD PRESS
205 NE BRYANT
PORTLAND, OR 97211

WWW.ERASERHEADPRESS.COM

ISBN: 978-1-62105-087-2

Copyright © 2013 by Jeff Burk

Cover art copyright © 2013 Hauke Vagt

Printed in the USA.

Acknowledgments

Super Huge Mega Thanks And Shout Outs To: Rose O'Keefe, Carlton Mellick III, Cameron Pierce, Kirsten Alene, Kevin Shamel, Chrissy Horchheimer, Hauke Vagt, Jon Horrid, Brian Keene, Rue Morgue Magazine, John Skipp, Cody Goodfellow, Veronica Chaos, Shane McKenzie, Edward Lee, Whitney Streed, Wrath James White, Tiffany Scandal, The H. P. Lovecraft Film Festival, Nate Southard, S. G. Brown, LeAnne Harden, The Lovecraft Bar, Ross E. Lockhart, that punk band that traded me drugs for a copy of *Bullet Through Your Face*, Erik Williams, Alan M. Clark, Garrett Cook, Effword, KillerCon, Bob Chaplin and everyone that travels to and helps out at BizarroCon.

Extra Belly Rubs To: the real-life Squishy:

BOOKS BY JEFF BURK

Shaterquake
Super Giant Monster Time!
Cripple Wolf
Shatnerquest
Lord of the LARPers
Homobomb
Pothead
The Slaughterhouse Thrills
Dinosaurs Attack
My Cat is a Camwhore!
Shatnerpocalypse

*This is dedicated to everyone
that's been bugging me for this book.
You wonderful weird and silly bastards.*

Author's Note

It's hard to believe that it's been four years since *Shatner-quake* came out. What started as a joke pitch from the high concept workshop at the first BizarroCon became a surprise bizarro success. It jump-started my writing career and afforded me so many opportunities that I would have otherwise never had. Wil Wheaton, Wesley Crusher himself, even gave *Shatnerquake* a shout-out. It makes me feel bad for making fun of Wesley for all those years...

I never expected so many people to enjoy a silly little book about William Shatner. And I certainly never imaged that I would write a sequel to it. Some of you might remember seeing *Shatnerquest* listed in the "also by" section in *Shatnerquake* but, at that time, it was purely a joke.

But then I had an idea for a trekkie road trip story.

When I wrote *Shatnerquake* I had just moved to Portland, Oregon from Pennsylvania and had just begun working for Eraserhead Press. At that time, Eraserhead was hitting the convention circuit pretty heavily (sometimes two a month) and the strange environment and the unique-to-those-events social interaction of nerds was my main inspiration. I was focusing on the ridiculous and absurd nature of fan culture.

But that was back in 2009 and a lot has changed since then. The past year was one of the most difficult years of my entire life. Vermin infestations, junkie housemates, failed relationships, and mysteriously losing the use of my right hand for a month (and then my left for another month) have been just *some* of the colorful events. But they're all stories for another time.

When I was a little kid, and things got really hard, I always retreated to the worlds of *Star Trek*, Godzilla movies, comic books, and video games. Still do. Sometimes it feels like the only thing that's changed is instead of just complimenting them with Mountain Dew and Goldfish crackers, I also have a bowl.

When it came time to write *Shatnerquest* I knew that's what I wanted to talk about. I wanted to focus about all the positives of fandom. How a sci-fi franchise can mend so many different wounds. How for so many people fandom has been the little light during the darkest of times.

So, come one. Life's shit, it's the end of the world, and the DeLorean's got one more empty seat.

Fuck it. Let's save William Shatner.

—Jeff Burk

PART 1

IN THE BEGINNING A BUNCH OF BAD SHIT HAPPENED

1
The World Did Not End With A Bang or a Whimper, But a Cheap Sound Effect

The apocalypse happened when Benny Russell was at SuperCoolCon. He was winning a *Magic: The Gathering* tournament.

It was Sunday, the third and final day of the convention celebrating comic books, video games, cosplaying, and all types of pop culture. The yearly event was an annual pilgrimage for any self-respecting geek within traveling distance of Baltimore, Maryland.

Being the last day, the tournament room had a good con-stink going on from the bodies of all the unwashed nerds. The large room was normally host to corporate meetings, but that day it was filled with a hundred people battling for the first prize of a limited edition two-foot-tall statue based on Brom's *Desolation Angel* card illustration.

It was his opponent's turn. A tall, obese man dressed as a Klingon. Benny knew him from his local gaming store. No matter where this guy went, he always wore his full costume (face ridges and all) and insisted on being called "Koloth." He even had a homemade cardboard bat'leth strapped to his back. On his lapel he wore a button that read, "I SPEED FOR TRIBBLES."

"Who's winning?" asked Gary.

"I'm at eighteen and Koloth's at twelve," said Benny, turning to face his best friend. Gary wore an Original Series Star Fleet uniform with the gold shirt for command. Benny also wore a Star Fleet uniform, but his was red for operations.

"Hey," shouted Koloth. "No helping."

"Fuck off you fat Klingon bastard," said Gary, flipping him the bird.

Koloth snorted and shoved some Cheetos into his mouth. He smeared orange cheese dust into the cheap metallic fabric of his specially-tailored costume and went back to studying his cards. Benny hated how Koloth always made you wait while he considered each move, as if he considered this game the height of intellectual play.

"You back already?" asked Benny. "I thought the movie didn't end for another hour."

"Fuck, dude," said Gary, "Whoever let Wes Anderson direct an *X-Men* sequel should be dragged into the street and shot. Wes Anderson, too."

A girl dressed as an elf stood up from the seat next to Benny, leaving the chair vacant.

"You wouldn't believe how much of a pussy Cyclops was."

"But you always think Cyclops is a pussy," Benny said, trying to ignore Koloth as the Klingon stuck his fat orange-stained fingers in his ear and then licked them clean.

Gary sat down in the vacant seat. "True, but the pussification is taken to a whole new level when you have Owen Wilson playing him."

Benny reached down and patted his fat cat Squishy. Her seventeen pounds of long white and brown fluff hadn't moved for the entire tournament. She snuggled up next to him wheezing—her weight had given her some breathing problems.

Benny took Squishy everywhere with him, carrying her around in a brown cloth satchel with a large Star Fleet insignia on the flap. Today she was wearing her own Star Fleet uniform, it was red and matched Benny's. It was meant for a baby, but fit the obese cat perfectly.

Squishy purred up at him and Gary reached down to pet her, too.

"How's Janice doing?"

"She's still in," Benny said, pointing across the room. "She's playing that loser."

Janice was seated across from a guy dressed as the Red Ranger from *Mighty Morphin Power Rangers*. The guy had gone the extra mile and had foam muscles on beneath the red lycra costume, making his body bulge with an unnaturally large physique just like a Rob Liefeld superhero.

12

The red ranger stood up and flexed his "biceps" in a body-builder pose.

"Doesn't look like it's going too good for her," said Gary.

Benny's eyes lingered on Janice. He loved the way she looked in her Star Fleet uniform. It was a classic female science officer's uniform. The short skirt showed off her toned thighs and the blue color matched her eyes.

"A-hem!" Koloth finished his turn.

Benny surveyed the battlefield, tapped one mountain, and cast Lightning Bolt. He laid down a card.

Koloth snorted, "I see you have the 2011 basic set." He was referring to the printing of the card. "I always use fourth edition or earlier. The art of Christopher Rush is far superior. Christopher Moeller really screwed it up in the reissue."

"Seriously dude?" Gary rolled his eyes.

"Someone with your taste probably doesn't even realize the difference."

"What's that supposed to mean?" asked Benny.

"You clearly care nothing for quality. You probably just bought the newer deck because it's cheaper."

Benny scowled, *you're such an asshat.*

"Your cards might be more expensive, but they aren't helping you win," said Benny.

"We'll see about that." Koloth snorted. "Are you done?"

"No," Benny grinned. "Not at all." He tapped three more mountains and two forests and was about to play the game finishing spell and put Koloth in his place.

Then it happened.

A voice boomed through the convention, "ATTENTION, ATTENTION WARP CORE BREACH IMMINENT."

Everyone paused from their games and looked around.

"I didn't know there was a speaker system," said Gary. "Did the LARPers get ahold of it?"

"That was Majel Barrett's voice," said Koloth. "But seriously, *cooome onnn.*"

"WARP CORE BREACH IMMINENT."

"Is there some kind of event or promotion going on?" asked Benny.

"There's nothing about it in the schedule," said Gary. "I'd be there instead."

"Hey, how's the game going?" said Janice walking over. She absent mindedly placed her hand on Benny's shoulder. He held his breath. He knew she didn't mean anything by it, but it didn't help the butterflies in his stomach.

"Pretty good," said Benny. "You out?"

"Yeah," she shrugged, "It hasn't been my day."

"Hey Janice," Koloth sneered. "Wanna come back to my place after the con? I'll even let you sit on my Throne of Bone?" He chuckled and snorted.

"Ugh," she said and ignored him.

Koloth licked his cheese encrusted lips at her and grabbed his crotch.

"Come on, man," said Benny disgusted.

"Ahhh, did I offend the white knight?"

"I'll never understand why you do the things that you do," said Gary. "But it could be all that corn syrup."

Koloth noisily slurped from a 2-liter bottle of Mt. Dew.

"Well, maybe Benny could finish his turn and then I'd have something else to distract myself," he said.

"Dude, there's still twelve minutes left to the round," said Gary, pointing at the clock. "He can take as long as he wants."

"ATTENTION, ATTENTION WARP CORE BREACH IMMINENT."

"What's with the announcements?" asked Janice.

"Don't know," said Benny. "I think it's for some kind of event."

"I wonder if it's for the new Star Trek movie?" mused Gary.

"I hope so," said Janice. "I would love a poster."

"Really? The remakes," Gary sighed. "They're a disgrace."

"We're not getting into this again," said Benny.

"For the love of god," said Koloth. "Finish your fucking turn."

They ignored him.

"WARP CORE BREACH IN 5 . . ."

The tournament room went quiet.

"4 . . ."

"What do you think is going to happen?" asked Janice.

Benny and Gary shrugged.

"3 . . ."

Some of the attendees began to join in with the countdown.

"Will you *please* finish you turn," Koloth squealed while rocking in his chair.

"2 . . ."

Benny, Gary, and Janice joined in counting down.

"1 . . ."

Everyone yelled along with the last number except Koloth, he was glaring at Benny.

A hush fell over the crowd as they waited to see what would happen. Everyone looked around at each other, but all the attendees had the same confused expressions. Then everyone resumed their matches.

"Well, that was anti-climactic," said Gary.

"Alright," said Benny turning his attention back to Koloth. He tapped his mana and held out one card. "You wanted me to finish? I hope you're ready for me to overrun your ass—"

The end of the world was heralded with a noise. The faithful heard trumpets. The skeptical heard an atomic blast. A few heard that killer riff from Slayer's "Angel of Death." The attendees of SuperCoolCon heard the deafening roar of an 8-bit explosion, like from an old NES game.

The whole convention center shook. The bright fluorescent lights flickered overhead. A tremor surged through the building and the statue at the front of the room toppled off the prize table and shattered when it hit the ground. The sudden crash caused someone to scream.

The building rocked once more, and somone screamed. A few started running to the exits.

"What's going on?" asked Gary.

"It sounded like an explosion," said Janice.

Benny stood up and grabbed Squishy. She squeaked as he shoved her into his satchel. He cradled the satchel to his chest as another 8-bit explosion shook the ground beneath them.

"We have to get out of here," said Benny.

Everyone else had already abandoned their games and was rushing for the exits.

Another 8-bit explosion happened and they joined the fleeing gamers.

"Hey," Koloth yelled behind them. "The game's not over!"

2
COMIC CON CATASTROPHE

Screaming bodies packed the lobby. Thick black smoke wafted through the air bringing the putrid stench of burnt plastic. Another boom rocked the building and the screaming mass surged forward. The glass revolving doors became jammed with limbs and costumes, allowing no one to escape.

"We can't get out this way," shouted Benny over the commotion.

Janice looked around, "Which way should we go?"

The crowd pushed again and Benny was pressed up against Janice. He smiled awkwardly at her but she wasn't paying attention to him. She watched a large woman in a Poison Ivy costume jump on top of a group of people and attempt to crowd surf toward the exit.

"Gary!"

Gary looked up at sound of his name.

"Gary . . . over here!"

It was a familiar voice.

He turned around and scanned the room. The convention center had televisions mounted high up on the walls that normally displayed advertisements for upcoming events or 24-hour news stations. For SuperCoolCon they were showing nonstop *Star Trek*.

A life-sized image of Captain Kirk stared straight out of the screen at Gary.

"Gary!" said Captain Kirk.

"Now's not really a good time," Gary shouted back.

"What was that?" asked Janice.

Gary shook his head at her and turned his attention back to the flat screen.

"You've got to . . . get out of here," said Captain Kirk from the television.

"But how?" asked Gary.

The crowd around them swayed back and forth, locking them in place. A man dressed as Thor tried to work his way through, swinging Mjolnir back and forth. He forgot that it was made of foam and it did nothing to open a way out. Against the back wall of the lobby was a young girl wearing pink fuzzy cat ears and a matching tail. She was splattered in something wet and red.

That looks like blood, thought Benny.

Something bad was happening. That was obvious but Benny could not see who Gary was addressing.

"Gary, who are you talking to?" he asked.

Gary waved him away.

"Gary," said Captain Kirk. "There's . . . a hallway . . . to the left of the lobby . . . and . . . an exit . . . through there. If you hurry you . . . can make it."

Gary nodded.

He turned to Benny and Janice. "Follow me," he shouted.

They forced their way along the back of the crowd to the left side of the lobby. Gary found the hallway Captain Kirk was talking about.

"Down there," he pointed.

A flaming boulder the size of a minivan burst through the front doors, shattering the glass and sending bodies into the air. It bounced, smashing through the wall, and hurdled into the auditorium where the *Magic* tournament had been happening minutes before.

The attendees surged with mindless panic in every direction. Benny saw a small man wearing a full body Spider-Man skin suit get sucked beneath the crowd. As Spidey went past, he heard the man shrieking and the snapping of breaking bones as he was trampled under hundreds of shoes.

Benny, Gary, and Janice ran down the side hallway. A few others had the same idea but most either didn't know about the alternate escape route or forgot in the panic.

Gary led the way and, just like the Captain said, there was an emergency exit. He pushed through the door with Benny and Janice close behind.

The sky above the convention was a swirling purple vortex. A large whirlpool filled the sky, where earlier there was peaceful blue. The edges of the spiral were bright neon purple and the phenomenon darkened to pitch black at the center. The darkness flashed bright white and spit out huge flaming boulders, smashing the hotel, the vehicles in the parking lot, and the surrounding area.

They ran through the parking lot zigzagging through wreckage and other fleeing con-goers.

"Watch out," shouted Benny. He grabbed Janice and yanked her aside.

A boulder slammed into the ground right where she had been standing and bounced away.

Janice gave him a grateful nod.

"Over here," said Gary, pointing. "I parked over here."

They ran down the parking aisle to where they had left Gary's mom's station wagon earlier in the day.

The poor car must have taken a direct hit. It was nothing more than a flat, smoldering heap of rubble, as if a steamroller had gone over top. If it wasn't for the brown and black paintjob they wouldn't have even been sure it *was* their station wagon.

"Fuck," screamed Gary. "Mom's gonna be pissed."

"What do we do now?" shouted Janice over the surrounding commotion.

Benny quickly glanced around. Some people had made it to working vehicles and were attempting to get away. Two cars collided head first in the parking lot exit, each trying to beat the other out. A third vehicle slammed into them, completely blocking off the exit and creating instant gridlock. Another fireball slammed down into the center of the mass of cars. Shrapnel flew through the air as the ball bounced.

The hotel was completely ablaze, and from the sounds emitting from it, there were many people still inside. Just a few hours ago it was one of the largest fan-conventions on the East Coast, now it was a flaming death trap.

Benny clutched Squishy tighter to his chest and he could feel her shaking.

"Guys," Gary shouted. "Guys! Snap out of it!"

Benny realized he had been lost watching the destruction. He turned to see what Gary was shouting about. As he did, he caught Janice's eyes. From the worry and blankness in her expression, he knew she was feeling the same way he was.

They faced Gary who had a big, broad smile. "Yo guys, let's steal the DeLorean."

He pointed at a shiny silver car, exactly the same as the one from *Back to the Future*. The creative modder had taken two small metal trash cans and welded them to the back with what looked like a lawn-mower engine mounted inbetween—a DIY time-travel capable jet-engine.

Gary took off for it and Benny and Janice followed.

"This is incredible" said Gary, stroking the side of the DeLorean.

"How the Hell are we going to steal it?" asked Benny, "And I think someone's gonna miss it."

"I wouldn't be so sure." Gary pointed to a red smear a few feet from the DeLorean. It took Benny a second to realize the smear use to be a human. All that was left un-mashed was part of a forearm with a hand holding a set of car keys.

Gary picked up the keys but the hand held on, dangling. He grimaced and grabbed the hand. With three hard tugs, he got it to let go and tossed the hand aside. He flashed Benny and Janice a smile and unlocked the DeLorean.

"Alright, let's go," he said to them while the door opened upwards and he hopped in the driver's seat.

Janice got in the passenger side and Benny and Squishy got in the back. They pulled forward and quickly saw that all the exits were just blockades of wreckage.

Gary put the car in reverse and backed down the parking lot.

"What are you doing?" screamed Janice.

"Cool down," he said. "I need some place to build up speed."

"What—" said Benny.

Gary shifted the gears and slammed the gas. The tires spun and squealed.

"Dudes, this is the DeLorean. We have to do this right," said Gary. He turned away and looked out the front windshield.

"But seriously, Hold on."

Gary shifted the car and they shot off. Benny and Janice lurched in their seats from the surge of speed, while Gary whooped and hollered.

He made a sharp turn at the end of the parking lane and the car slid. The tires screamed. Gary righted them and the DeLorean rocketed forward. Ahead of them was the end of the parking lot—a grassy knoll, the sidewalk, and then the highway. Gary gunned the engine and the DeLorean purred as they picked up even more speed. They hit the curb and the car bounced. It violently rocked and they went over the grass and then slammed into the sidewalk.

As they hit the asphalt of the highway, they swerved a few times, but Gary regained control and sped away from the convention. Benny turned and looked out the back window. The convention center was fully engulfed in flames as boulders continued falling from the sky. It didn't look like too many other cars were making it out.

Benny turned around and leaned back in the plush interior. He started petting Squishy who was looking up at him with big green eyes.

They turned on the car's CD player and a disc kicked in that the previous owner must have been listening to, it was the theme to *Star Trek: the Original Series*.

3
IT'S THE END OF THE WORLD
AS WE KNOW IT
(AND I FEEL NERDY)

"What the fuck was that all about?" said Janice.

They were speeding down the highway. The road was, for the most part, empty. At one point a wailing police car sped past them and they saw a blaring ambulance heading the other direction, but they seemed to have the road to themselves.

"I don't know but I can't get anything on my phone. No service at all," Benny said from the backseat. "Anything on the radio?"

"Nope," said Janice and she turned the nob. All they were picking up was static. "Nothing at all."

"I got an idea," said Gary.

"Terrorists," said Janice from the back.

"Hey, that makes sense," said Benny. "Our phones aren't working, the radio's out. Like an EMP blast."

"It's not terrorists and it's definitely not an EMP. This car wouldn't be working if that was the case. And what terrorist would want to attack SuperCoolCon? We're not exactly a politically powerful voting block."

"Then what do you think it is?" asked Janice.

"Dimensional gateways," he said.

"What?"

"That weird swirling purply thingy in the sky? That was a gateway to another dimension. Those rocks falling through was that world leaking into our own."

"That's stupid," said Janice.

"Well whatever it is," said Benny trying his phone again, "we'll know more soon. It should only be another fifteen minutes until we're home. I'm sure once we're around a computer we'll know more."

***

They saw the smoke from several miles away. A thick blanket of black soot poured into the sky.

"That's Stewartstown, isn't it?" said Janice.

"Yep," said Benny. "The next exit is the overlook. Gary, pull over there."

"Aye, aye, Captain."

The DeLorean pulled off the highway and parked. Benny, Gary, Janice, and Squishy climbed out and saw their town engulfed in flames. Large beasts, the things of myths and movies, moved through the burning haze, toppling buildings and eating people.

"Doesn't that look like Godzilla?" Janice said while pointing.

"Yeah, and I'm pretty sure that's the Stay Puft Marshmallow Man over there," replied Benny as he lit up a cigarette.

"What the fuck?" said Janice.

"See, I told you," said Gary. "Dimensional vortex. But it's from our minds, like in a Grant Morrison comic or like the end of *Ghostbusters*. Some asshole was watching the DVD as the next moment, *poof*, Stay Puft is stomping on the Rutter's."

"Do you know how crazy that sounds?"

"Crazier things have happened."

"No they haven't!"

"Guys," shouted Janice. "Focus . . . Stewartstown . . . it's gone."

"We know that," said Gary. "But—"

"No," she said. "Stop and think about it." She turned and gazed out, "It's gone. Or, it will be soon."

They looked out in stunned silence as their home burned to the ground. None of them really liked the place, it was a shitty small town with nothing ever going on. But it was still their home. Where they lived and played and worked— where they had built what passed for a life. And now it was being reduced to smoldering rubble before their eyes.

The air was harsh and stank of burning wood, rubble, concrete, and metal. It stung their eyes and made it hard to breathe. Squishy rolled around on the pavement, wheezing, and stopped to cough.

"Dudes," said Gary, breaking the silence. "Godzilla really fucked up Original's Pizza. Where the hell am I going to grab a slice now?"

"I really think there's bigger things to worry about right now," said Janice.

"Like what?"

"Like the fact that it looks like Godzilla's headed in the direction of your neighborhood right now," said Benny, pointing.

"He might veer off . . ." said Gary.

Through the smoke of the burning town they saw the silhouette of the giant lizard leveling businesses and homes. The monster's scales glowed bright blue and the beast's mouth was illuminated with the same unearthly light. A beam shot out from its gaping maw and blasted through Gary's neighborhood, leaving fiery explosions in its wake.

"Never mind," said Gary.

He watched his house go up in flames.

"So . . ." said Janice. "What do we do now?"

"We could go look for Vash, he might—" Gary started to suggest.

"We broke up last night."

"Really?" Benny sounded surprised. "What—"

"I don't want to talk about it."

Again, a heavy silence came down on them.

"Well," said Benny, "does anyone have any friends or family that they want check in on?"

"We could see if your dad's okay, Gary," said Janice.

"Shit, no," said Gary.

"Janice, what about you?" asked Benny

"My parents and sister are in Portland," said Janice.

"Right . . . I got nothing." said Benny.

"Do you want to go get anything from your place?" asked Janice.

"Don't really think that's an option," he said pointing. "Looks like my building's going up like the convention center." His apartment building was engulfed in flames and, if that wasn't bad enough, a giant monster was fucking it.

The creature had the body of a centipede and claws like a lobster's. The thing was grinding against the building and shaking it apart. Its claws gripped the sides of the building and its pelvis bashed at the structure.

"In fact, I think my apartment building might be getting it worse. What about yours?"

She shook her head. "No, there's nothing I want to get from there."

"We could go loot the shopping mall?" suggested Gary.

"Nah," said Janice. "I'm not really into that whole joining the mindless rioting masses kinda thing."

"I got it," said Gary as he snapped his fingers and a huge smile crept across his face. "Let's save William Shatner."

"What?" said Janice.

"Let's fucking save William Shatner," said Gary. "If we don't save him who will?"

Janice was flabbergasted. She didn't know how to answer that.

"Come on," continued Gary. "We just learned that we don't have anyone looking for us and there's no one for us to look for. What the fuck else are we going to do, just sit here with our thumbs up our asses?

"Look," Gary pointed at Janice, Benny, and Squishy, "William Shatner could need us right now. His life could depend on us. Can you live with yourself?"

"How could we even find him?" asked Janice attempting to bring some rationality back into the debate.

"He's in L.A."

"How can you be sure?"

"He was posting on twitter earlier today about how the filming of his cameo scenes for the new *Star Trek* movie are going. Personally, I think it's beneath him, but his schedule has him in California for the next week."

"That's kinda creepy that you know that."

"That's not the point. We can save him. You said it yourself, Janice. You didn't want to join in with the mindless masses or whatever. We could do *something*."

"Where would he be in L.A. anyway?" said Benny.

"He's got a house in Beverly Hills and the shoot's happening on a Paramount Studios sound stage, so he's got to be somewhere around there."

"But why William Shatner? Why not . . . Bruce Campbell or Adam West?" asked Janice.

"Because Bruce can take care of himself and fuck Adam West," said Gary. "Why William Shatner? Because it's Captain fucking Kirk and it's the apocalypse, who else would you want by your side?"

Janice turned to Benny for help. "Would you please say something?"

"I'm in," said Benny, snuffing out his cigarette.

"What?" Janice couldn't believe what she heard.

"Look," continued Benny. "We don't know what's going on, our phones aren't working, and we haven't come across any place that isn't being utterly fucked in the ass yet. We need to at least try to get someplace where everything isn't going to shit. Heading west is as good a plan as anything." He shrugged. "I got Squishy and at the very least I've never been to L.A."

"That's the spirit," exclaimed Gary. He turned to Janice. "He's got a point. We can't just stay here. It looks like Stewartstown is, at the very least, a major disaster zone. What else do you want to do?"

"I'm okay with heading west looking for help but I don't know about saving William Shatner. If this is as bad as you think it is, what makes you think he's even alive?"

"I *know* he is. He's a rich celebrity so if anyone is going to be able to protect themselves it's going to be him. He's probably locked up in some kinda safe room right now."

"Then why would he need us anyway?"

"Because he's going to be by himself. It's the end of the world. Do you think his body guards are going to be sticking around? If you thought it was the end would you keep doing your crappy job? No. We can go there and get him out."

"But what then?"

Gary shook his fists. "I don't know. I admit, I don't have this completely thought out but somewhere right now William Shatner is by himself and he needs somebody."

Janice shook her head and walked away from Gary and Benny to the edge of the overlook. Giant tentacles burst from beneath the city streets, snatching up escaping cars, and pulling them underground to some unknown fate. In the distance, she could see something that looked like a Pterodactyl swooping against the clouds.

She turned back to Gary and Benny who were both watching her, waiting for her answer.

"Fuck it. Let's save William Shatner."

4
THE CHAPTER THAT'S LIKE A KEVIN SMITH MOVIE

Benny picked up Squishy and they walked back to the DeLorean.

"We don't have anything for the trip," He said. "I don't know about you guys, but I was planning on grabbing dinner after the tournament. Doesn't look like that's going to happen now . . ."

"We can hit up the Safeway out in Shrewsbury. Grab some supplies for our trip while we're there," suggested Janice.

"Nah, fuck that," said Gary. "You've seen how the stores get when there's a snow storm. What do you think giant monsters attacking is going to look like?"

"So what do you suggest?"

"Brave Nerd World."

"Why the hell do you want to get comic books right now?" asked Benny.

"No," said Gary. "But in the gaming room there's that stand with all the snacks and soda. It's as good as any gas station. Plus they have beer. And it's about two miles over there," he said pointing. "None of the monsters have made it there yet or are even headed that way."

"That should hold us over," said Benny.

He looked at Janice and she nodded. "It'll work until we find something better."

Benny picked up Squishy and they walked to the car.

"This better not be because you want to check your pull-box," said Janice to Gary as they got in.

***

"Sweet, the new issue of *Crossed* is out," said Gary, as he pulled the stack of comic books out of slot 737—his pull-box for the past couple years. "Guys, new *Action Comics, Mars Attacks,* and *Star Trek: The Next Generation/Doctor Who: Assimilation.*"

"You asshole," said Janice.

"Hello," Benny called out into the store.

The front door was unlocked and they had just walked right in. The lights were out in the store and flicking the switches did nothing.

"Who's supposed to be working today?" asked Benny.

"Uh, it's Sunday," said Gary. "Jason should be on."

"Not like him to flake out," said Janice.

"There are big fucking monsters out there," said Gary as he pulled out plastic bags from behind the counter and handed them to Benny and Janice.

"Yeah, but why'd he leave the door open?" asked Benny.

He lifted Squishy out of his bag and set her down on the floor. She waddled over to a cat food dish with the words "frakin feed me" engraved on the side. It was in her usual spot beside the counter.

Gary shrugged. "Don't know. We can leave an IOU."

There was a TV mounted above the checkout. Gary tried turning it on and nothing happened. He cursed under his breath, slapped the side of the TV and tried again. Nothing.

"Fuck," he shouted.

"You know there's no power," said Janice.

She picked up a light saber keychain from a display on the counter top and pressed the button that made it light up. It emitted a weak green light. She frowned and tossed it back down.

The store was one large, long space. The front third was rows of board games and glass cases filled with rare *Magic: the Gathering* cards and Warhammer figures. Racks of new comics lined the middle of the store. The back area was tables for gaming events plus the store's snacks and bar. They walked to the back of the store to get the food and drink.

"If this is really the end of the world I sure as hell am going to miss TV," said Gary.

"You might have a bit of an addiction there," said Benny, as he filled a bag with Nintendo gummies, star wars Pez and freeze dried ice cream.

"No, seriously," said Gary. "It's really gotten me through a lot. I'm not sure what I'm going to do without it." He was loading 22s of IPA into a bag.

"God you're right, I really am going to miss TV," said Janice. "There's going to be no more *Game of Thrones*."

Gary laughed. "I knew George R. R. Martin was never going to finish those books."

"We're never going to get another Jodorowsky movie," said Benny.

"No more *Doctor Who*," lamented Janice.

"Didn't I read that Tarantino was working on the next Batman movie?" said Benny. "I wonder how that would have turned out?"

Gary snorted. "Half the scenes would be shot-for-shot rip-offs of Sergio Leone—the other half Kurosawa, Batman would get into an argument with the Joker over eighties pop music, and the final battle with Killer Croc would have Wu-Tang Clan as the soundtrack."

"That would have been awesome."

"Yeah . . ."

"I'm going to miss the internet," said Janice. "No more Angry Video Game Nerd, no more The Guild, no more Idea Channel."

"No more Red Versus Blue," said Benny. "Or BoingBoing, Gawker, Toplessrobot, PostSecret, or Lolcats. Hell, it's not just the internet. Radio's not even working. With all the driving we're going to be doing I wish we could listen to Coast to Coast A.M.."

"This is getting depressing."

"You know what I'm not going to miss," said Janice cutting in, "Furries."

"Bronies," said Benny.

"*Twilight* fans and *Twilight* haters," added Janice.

"No more *Star Trek* remakes," said Gary.

"Oh come on," said Benny. "They're not that bad."

"Lensflare! Lensflare! Lensflare!" shouted Gary.

"Dubstep is dead," said Janice.

"Hopefully, Brokencyde too," said Benny.

"Everyone ever involved with *The Big Bang Theory*. Or anyone who likes the show."

"No more George Fucking Lucas," yelled Gary with his hands raised in devil horns.

They all laughed. This was actually a lot of fun. They had lost their homes but they had an adventure ahead and they had each other.

They took the first load of goods out to the car.

"So what do you think Shatner's doing now?" asked Janice as they walked back in.

"Probably chillin' out and waiting for some brave adventurers like us to come to his aid," said Gary. He picked up a porcelain Harley Quinn statue.

"What the hell are you going to do with that?" asked Janice.

Gary looked at her shocked, "We're looting. You can't expect me not to take advantage of that. I need to get something cool."

"But what the fuck are you going to do with a statue in the car?"

"Okay," he said and put Harley Quinn back down. "But I'm going to steal some trade paperbacks. It's a long drive, we'll need reading material."

"Good thinking," said Benny. "I've been wanting that *Howard the Duck* omnibus."

Janice shrugged and smiled. "While you boys take care of that, I'm going to use the bathroom."

She walked through the store to the bathrooms in the back. A wooden door with a male/female sign marked the single occupancy restroom. She pushed open the door and shrieked.

Hanging from the bathroom ceiling was Jason with a noose around his neck and his pants around his ankles. The rope was pulled tight and his skin was turning purple. His eyes bulged out of his face and his bloated tongue stuck out.

31

His naked penis was still erect. His body gently swayed back and forth.

"Holy shit," said Gary. He and Benny came running up next to Janice, their arms full of comic books and trade paperbacks.

"So that's what happened to Jason," said Benny.

"That's the limited edition Wonder Woman lasso," said Gary pointing to the rope wrapped around the dead man's neck. "That's worth like seventy-five dollars. Asshole."

"I'm pissing in the alley," said Janice shutting the door.

***

Janice came around the corner wiping her hands on the side of her costume.

Benny was smoking a cigarette against the DeLorean and looking off into the distance where black smoke continued to pour into the sky. There were vague shapes that moved around in the darkness but they were too far away to make out—thank god.

Gary was pouring over a roadmap he had unfolded in his hands.

"Hey," said Janice. "What you looking at there?"

"Found some maps in the glove compartment," said Gary. "Figuring out the best way to get to L.A."

"So we're really serious about this?" said Janice.

"Fuck yeah we are," said Gary. "We're gonna have this fucking golden."

"Heading west is a good idea," said Benny taking another drag as something roared in the distant smoke.

"And looking over these maps, I got a good idea," said Gary. "What do you all say we head west for like two hundred miles and then go a little north for a brief detour in Riverside, Iowa?"

"Riverside, Iowa?" said Benny.

"Yeah, it's just three hundred miles away. It's really not far out of our way, just like an hour or two extra."

"What's in Riverside?" asked Janice.

"The birthplace of Captain James T. Kirk."

"I'm okay with a little detour," said Benny.

They got into the DeLorean and pulled out of the parking space on the side of the street. The car lurched and sputtered.

"Fuck," said Benny. "This car's a piece of shit. I wish there had been a Batmobile for us to steal."

5
THE ROAD WARRIOR'S BATHROOM BREAK

"Dude, there's like . . . an ounce of weed back here!"

Benny and Janice rested on a nearby bench while Squishy waddled around in the grass. Gary had been digging through the trunk hoping to find anything useful. He didn't find anything special until he checked the spare tire compartment. That's where he found the marijuana.

"Oh yeah," said Benny.

"Yep. There's even rolling papers," said Gary, shutting the trunk and moving from behind the car. He was holding up a clear plastic bag filled with green buds. "I'd say we got enough to make it to L.A."

He rolled them a joint and the three passed it around. They were somewhere in Ohio and the sun was beaming down. A slightly cool breeze passed through the rest stop. The tall trees swayed back and forth. On the highway, it was easy to forget the devastation happening elsewhere.

"This is like that scene in that road trip movie," said Gary.

"Which one?" said Janice.

"All of them," he said passing her the joint. "It's not a proper road trip story until all the heroes have set out on their adventure and there's the scene where they're taking in the quest and sharing a smoke or a drink. *Fear and Loathing in Las Vegas*, *Detroit Rock City*, *Easy Rider*—they all have that scene."

"Yeah, but what happens after those scenes?" said Benny.

He looked down at Squishy. She was no longer frolicking but hunched down, her fur ruffled and ears back, staring down the highway. There was a low rumble that gradually grew louder.

"Do you hear that?" he asked.

"Yeah," said Gary. "What is that?"

"Motorcycles," said Janice.

Gary jammed the big bag of weed down the front of his pants. Benny kept smoking the joint.

"You should put that out," said Janice.

"Just play it cool," he said. "No one's going to care about someone smoking a joint right now."

The sounds of the bikes got louder and then five people on motorcycles crested the hill. The bikes drove in tight formation. Their leader was very obese. The bikes turned at the off-ramp for the rest stop and pulled up next to the DeLorean.

The four bikers got off their bikes and walked up to Benny, Gary, and Janice sitting on the bench. Their leader stayed in the back.

"What have we here," said one of the bikers. He was sickly skinny with open oozing sores around his mouth. In the center of his forehead was a rubber prosthetic Klingon ridge piece. All the bikers were wearing the forehead pieces.

"Holy shit," said another biker with a green mohawk. His arms were decorated with iron crosses and swastikas. "They're in Star Fleet outfits. Was there a convention I missed?"

"Well yeah," said Gary. He pointed to his forehead, "and you got the—"

"Shut up," said the third biker. His eyebrows were shaved away and his face tattooed with arcane symbols and tribal patterns, a spider-web covered his shaved head.

"He's right," said Benny. "Those are Klingon ridges."

"He said shut-up," said the fourth biker. A Hispanic man with long black hair pulled back in a pony-tail, black shades, and a big black mustache. He was dressed head to toe in black leather.

"Awww, look at the cat," said the mohawked biker. "It's got a little uniform too." The man practically squealed the last part.

"And you can shut up too," said the biker with the face tattoos. "You're not helping."

"Of all people to meet out here, I didn't expect you

three," said a familiar voice. The bikers parted a path for their leader.

Gary rolled his eyes, "You've got to be kidding me."

"Glad to see you're not dead," said Koloth. He now had a leather jacket on over his Klingon armor. "And especially glad to see you made it Janice."

He reached out and stroked her cheek with his chubby finger.

"Don't fucking touch me," said Janice, flinching away from him.

"You know her, boss?" snickered the biker with long hair. "She's mighty fine."

"I'll say," said the face-tattooed biker.

"Boys, boys," said Koloth. "Calm yourselves. Act with honor."

"So where'd you find the new friends?" said Benny.

"Oh," smiled Koloth. "It's a thrilling story I assure you, but it should wait until later." He gestured with his head to the DeLorean. "Where'd you get that?"

"Found it outside the convention," answered Gary. "Isn't it amazing?"

Koloth rubbed his hands over the hood. "Amazing, indeed. Definitely not a sale model but custom made to resemble the movie's version." He crouched down with great difficulty. "Took some damage I see. Not mint." He grunted and stood back up. "You really should take better care of your collectibles."

Koloth smiled a toothy grin. His teeth were rotten from years of junk-food, soda, and being too "in-the-zone" while gaming to brush. Benny thought he really did look like a Klingon.

"So where are you carnival of losers headed?"

"We're going to save William Shatner," Gary said.

Koloth started to laugh and the other bikers joined in.

"William Shatner?" repeated Koloth. "*You're* going to save William Shatner? He's where? L.A.?"

"That's the idea," said Janice.

Benny passed Gary the joint and the mohawked biker

darted forward and snatched it from his hand. He took a big hit and then passed it to the skinny biker.

"Yeah, that's cool I guess," said Gary sitting back and crossing his arms. "Help yourself."

"And I see you still have that cat with you." Koloth leaned down to pet Squishy but she hunched back and hissed. "Fucking cat."

"What do you want, Koloth?" said Benny staring him in the eyes.

"Depends. What do you got?"

"I want the girl," said the skinhead biker. He was leering at Janice, his eyes locked on her thighs. She nervously tried to pull the skirt further down. The other bikers chuckled. "She's mighty fine split-tail, she'd do us well."

Benny saw a flash of doubt and worry flash across Koloth's eyes. He wasn't expecting that.

Koloth quickly regained his leadership composure, "They do have a point my dear Janice." He moved closer to her. "I am building a great army and I am currently in need of a queen. What do you say? Will you ride by my side?"

Janice crossed her arms. "Never. Why would you think I'd have any interest in being around you? You're a pervy asshole."

The bikers snickered. "Bitch gots a mouth," one of them said.

Koloth glared at her.

"Tear their car apart," Koloth shouted back at his men without taking his eyes off of them. "Take anything that might be of use."

The bikers sneered at Janice but they moved back to the DeLorean.

Gary leapt to his feet, "What the fuck you assholes think—"

His words froze when the biker in black leather stepped forward, flicked his wrist, and held an eight inch switch-blade to Gary's throat.

"You're just going to want to sit there and wait for us to finish," said Koloth. "My crew can get a little carried away."

The bikers dug through the seats, compartments, and

trunk. While Koloth and the leather-clad biker with the knife stood watch over Benny, Janice, and Gary.

Benny picked up Squishy and placed her in his lap. She hissed at the bikers.

The bikers finished their search and the skinny biker walked over to Koloth.

"Anything?" asked Koloth.

"A whole bunch of shit—food, beer, soda, a whole bunch of other comic books."

"Comic books?" said Koloth raising his eyebrow.

"Yeah, a whole bunch of them. What do you want done with the shit?"

"Take all the food and drink and load it up. Bring the comics over here."

The bikers quickly took everything they had raided from Brave Nerd World and loaded it onto their bikes.

The skinny biker brought over the comic books and threw them in a pile on the ground.

"Where'd you get all the comics?" asked Koloth.

"Made a stop on the way out of town," said Gary.

"You stole these too? Tsk tsk." Koloth turned to the biker with the knife. "Do you have a lighter?"

"Sure do boss."

"Excellent. On my signal would you be so kind to set that pile of pulp trash aflame?"

"Will do."

Benny, Gary, and Janice all groaned.

"Seriously," said Janice. "You're an asshole."

"You only get one," he said with vile in his voice. "You better hope not to see me again. Next time," he looked Janice up and down, "I might not be so gracious. Light 'em up."

The biker flicked the lighter at the corner of the comic pile. It took a moment for them to catch but once the flame got started, the pile of bound paper was quickly ablaze.

"Oh, that's just a dick move," said Gary.

Koloth spit on the ground and got on his bike. "Remember, only one."

His bike purred to life and he sped out of the rest stop,

the other bikers followed suit.

Squishy hissed.

They were quiet for a moment and then Gary said, "Stupid fucking shit."

He reached into his pants and pulled out the big bag of weed. There were already several pre-rolled joints. He pulled one out and went over to the small bonfire that had been their comic stash. He picked up a flaming page, it looked to be from *Swamp Thing*, and held it in front of his face. The flame lit the joint and he puffed out white smoke.

"At least they didn't search us. Who could go for a hit?"

6
BENNY RUSSELL'S STORY

Last night:
Benny stepped into his studio apartment and shut the door. Before even setting down the bag, he flipped the two deadbolts. On his way down the hall leading to his room he heard two couples fighting, one, judging from the smacking sounds, coming to blows, a baby crying, and at least three people screaming at their own demons.

Once he shut the door, all the sounds of personal torment went silent. At least the building had good soundproofing.

His apartment was a wreck but, in all fairness, it was pretty hard to keep clean considering how small it was. If he didn't tidy up right away, it went to shit. Books, beer cans, and cigarette butts littered the floor.

It wasn't much but it suited him. There was a twin-sized bed, a desk for his laptop, a sink, two bookcases, a small personal-sized fridge, and room for nothing else. The bathroom was one common toilet in a room at the end of the hallway for the fifteen people that lived on the floor.

He opened the fridge, and put in the beer he had just bought—two six-packs of PBR—inside. He pulled one off the plastic rings and cracked it open.

"Me-row?" Squishy was waddling over and Benny smiled at her. Her picked up the bag of cat food from on top of the fridge and filled up her bowl underneath the sink.

Six years ago:
Benny was sitting in front of his computer and could not believe the email. He had worked for six months straight on *Killing Kittens for Fun and Profit.* The long nights of coding had almost killed him but the game was finally out and down. Just earlier that day it had come out via Xbox Live and the

PlayStation Network.

The email from his distributor said that the game had sold a total of ten thousand copies on its first day.

Ten thousand.

This was it. Finally the reward from all the years of struggling and all the hard work. This was going to change everything.

He called Si, his girlfriend, to tell her the good news.

Five years ago:

Excerpt from an interview originally published on the website *Gamer Nerds Gossip:*

Gamer Nerds Gossip: *Killing Kittens for Fun and Profit* may be one of the most exciting and original indie games in years, what is next for you?

Benny Russell: I can't express how happy it has made me over how well players have reacted to my game. Truly it is a dream come true. They made me and they are in the forefront of my mind for my next game. I can't talk too much about it yet. But I can tell you the title, *Super Mega Space Badger Jam.*

GNG: Sounds sweet. When can we expect it?

BR: It will be out this time next year.

Four years ago:

Benny was sitting in front of his computer in the modest one bedroom apartment that he rented with Si. He typed code furiously, his fingers a blur. He was really just hitting keys, there was so many errors in what he was typing that there was no way it could work. But that didn't matter—he just needed to keep himself busy.

The walls around him were barer than normal. There used to be many pieces of artwork and posters of events covering them but Si had taken a lot of them.

She walked to the front door with her last two bags. This was her final load and she would be gone for good.

"I hope you finish that game," she said.

Benny didn't respond. He just kept typing.

"Yeah," she said and left.

Three years ago:
The short fat bald man chomped on the cigar and unlocked the door.

"Yeah, there's not much to it. A bed, a desk, some shelves, fridge, sink, bathrooms' in the hall."

Benny stepped in and looked around. The room was small and looked like a flophouse from the nineteen twenties but it would suit his needs. He just wanted someplace to work. The money from his first game was starting to run thin and there was no way he could continue to afford the place that Si and he used to share. It was not nearly as nice, a major step down, but it would be a place to work until things got going again. He was behind on his game but if he just had a place to work he knew he could get it done.

"I'll take it."

Two years ago:
Benny logged into his email. There were twenty new messages since the last time he checked. Nineteen of them were from gamers, irrationally pissed off, demanding the release date for *Super Mega Space Badger Jam*. One of them was even from that asshole at the comic store that never took off his Klingon makeup.

The twentieth email was from his distributor, angry about how he was three months late on his fifth extension.

His hands hovered above the keyboard but Benny just could not bring himself to respond. He marked all the emails as READ and closed the internet. He considered working on the game more that night but decided instead to crack open a beer and watch some *South Park* reruns online.

He wanted to work that night. He really did. But his mind and hands felt paralyzed. He drank until he didn't think about it anymore.

One year ago:
Benny was hanging out in Brave Nerd World, his favorite comic and gaming store in town when she walked in. He heard the ding of the door opening and turned to see who

it was, hoping for maybe one of his *Magic* or D&D friends when she walked in.

She had long dark hair and high cheek bones. Her eyes were dark and she wore a shirt with a screen-printed Star Trek insignia on the front. He felt like he was punched in the gut when he saw her.

She wandered through the store and got noticeably interested when she saw a section of Grant Morrison trade-paperbacks. She pulled out a copy of *The Filth* and started flipping through it.

Benny debated if he should say anything and after a few minutes of working up the courage he walked over to her.

"Hi, I'm Benny. You a Grant Morrison fan?"

She looked up at him with big dark brown eyes. There was a momentary flash of suspicion across her face and then it softened.

"Yeah," she said. "He's my favorite writer." She held out her hand. "I'm Janice."

Six months ago:
"Dude, you should totally make a move," said Gary.

Benny shuffled his deck and looked over at Janice. She was playing that asshole Koloth this round.

"I don't know," he said. "I really don't think she's into me."

"Yeah sure," Gary snorted as he dealt out his hand. "She's been coming with us to tournament nights for, what, three months? And coming out drinking after? I see how she talks to you. Dude, she's totally into you."

"I really don't think so, I think you're being overly optimistic."

"And you're being a scared little bitch. It's the same reason your game's not done yet."

Benny glared at him. "You're one to talk."

"Dude, I just calls 'em as I sees 'em."

Three months ago:
Benny and Janice were sitting at the bar next to each other. They had traveled down to Baltimore for the *Planeshift*

expansion prerelease tournament. They had lately been getting into the habit of going out for special events, just the two of them, and then grabbing many beers late into the evening afterwards.

"I've been having a lot of fun hanging out with you lately," said Benny.

"I have too," Janice smiled at him. "The tournament today was pretty fun but I just wish I drew better cards."

"Yeah, I got hosed too," said Benny. "But there's something else I wanted to talk to you about. I've been having a lot of fun with you and I think you're a really cool person. I . . . I was wondering if you'd like to go out on a date sometime?"

"Oh," said Janice. Her smile dropped and she looked away.

"Shit," said Benny and took a swig of his beer. "I'm sorry I fucked this up. I—"

"No, no," she said. "It's not that. I . . . I really like you but you caught me at a . . . bad time."

"Oh."

"I'm . . . I'm engaged."

Today:
Gary: Yo, dude. I'm outside.

Benny texted back "I'll be right out" and chugged the end of the beer while Squishy rolled around at his feet. He stood up and made sure he had his bag packed—comics and DVDs for the guests to sign, some weed, and his *Magic* deck. Alright, he was ready to go.

He texted Janice that they would be on their way to pick her up. He didn't understand why she was with that Vash guy. He didn't like any of the things that she did. But Janice said they were in love and they were getting married. Not like there was anything he could do about it now.

He got back a text from Janice, "OK, see you soon."

He put on his backpack and slung his satchel over his side. He picked up Squishy, who purred loudly, and placed her in the satchel. He headed out the door, kicking over a few beer cans in the process.

Well, if this was the only way he was going to see Janice that would be the way it had to be. He locked his door and headed down to the car. Soon he would see Janice again and today was the first day of SuperCoolCon.

It had to be a good day. He really needed one of those.

7
WAIT, THE BORG ARE IN THIS BOOK?

The dead body slowly stood up. It swayed on shaky feet and turned its head, looking around the scene of the accident. Its right eye had been knocked out of its socket and was dangling on the corpse's cheek. It took a weak step and its intestines unfurled from the gaping wound in its stomach.

The man, or what use to be a man, shambled over to the overturned truck, its guts dragging on the ground. The vehicle had smashed into a tree, ejecting the unfortunate driver through the windshield. The mangled frame was still smoking and the engine hissed.

The walking corpse picked up a piece of piping that had broken off the truck. It raised the metal to the empty eye socket and began to push it in the hole. The pipe first met resistance but then the eye socket bone broke and flesh tore. The pipe slid into place, severing the optic nerve and the ruined eye plopped to the ground.

"This is so fucked-up," said Gary.

They were somewhere in the middle of Indiana and had taken an exit with signs for gas and food. They had been on the road for three days and, after the bikers had stolen everything, they were running dangerously low on what food and water they had managed to salvage from other vehicles on the road.

Once off the highway, they found themselves in farm country and had come across the wrecked truck.

"Pull over," said Janice. "I think I see someone moving."

They did and that's when the body stood up and began self-mutilation. The corpse had now moved to the smoking engine and pulled out a wire. It inserted one torn end in the bicep of its right arm and then hooked the other end in the flesh attached to its hand. The corpse dug into the engine for more parts.

"Should we stop it?" asked Janice.

"No," said Benny. "I really think we should just let it be."

The three of them stood in a row watching the thing elaborately decorate its body with machine parts. Squishy had been left inside the DeLorean and she had her face and paws pressed against the window. She let out a low growl at the corpse.

The corpse suddenly stood up straight and turned to face them. It began to walk towards them with jerky movements. Not like it was a banged-up zombie but more like a person pretending to be a robot.

"We are the Borg," it said with a dry, monotone voice.

"You have got to be fucking with me," said Gary.

"Alright," Benny flicked his cigarette to the ground, "I think it's time we find that gas station."

They quickly got into the car. Benny hopped in the driver's side and turned the keys but nothing happened. He turned them again but nothing happened.

"Benny," said Gary, "Let's get going."

The Zombie Borg was just a few feet from the car. "We are the Borg. We are the Borg. We are the Borg."

"I'm trying," said Benny. "The fucking car's not working."

He turned the key two more times and the engine tried to roll over but did not start.

He hit the dashboard. "Fucking bitch."

The Zombie Borg was now next to the DeLorean. It raised one bloody arm and began to bang on the window next to Gary.

"Dude," he said. "We really need to go."

Benny took the keys out of the ignition and rubbed them in his hands. He closed his eyes and tried to ignore the banging. He put the keys back in and turned. The engine roared to life.

"Fuck yeah," he yelled.

Benny put the car into drive and they took off. Gary looked out the back window and flipped off the Zombie Borg now wandering in the center of the road.

47

***

Five minutes down the road, they came upon the gas station the highway signs had promised. It was a desolate corner surrounded by tall corn fields. It was one of those gas stations with a large fueling lot and a full convenience store.

They pulled up to one of the pumps and they all got out except for Squishy. They looked around but there were no other cars or sounds of anyone or anything nearby. The wind blew through and rustled the corn.

"It's awfully . . . quiet," said Janice.

"I know," said Benny as he went to the pump.

The LCD display was still working and he put the nozzle into the DeLorean's gas inlet. Benny hit PAY INSIDE and the gas starting flowing.

He smiled. "We're in business."

"I'm going to go check inside," said Gary.

"I'll come with you," said Janice and she followed.

The store was fully stocked and seemed undisturbed— aisles of snack foods, car supplies, and basic needs like batteries and aspirin, plus a freezer of drinks.

"Oh god, what is that?" asked Gary, covering his nose.

"Smells like something died in here," said Janice.

"Fuck it," said Gary. He went to the candy aisle and started grabbing sweets and shoving them in his pocket.

Janice moved slowly forward, continuing to scan the store. She looked at the unmanned check-out counter and something struck her as odd. It took a moment, and then she noticed the specks of rust-red dotting the wall of cigarettes behind it. She moved carefully down the counter to the corner where the attendant should be.

On the ground behind the counter was what used to be a person. The body was spilt from neck to groin and everything inside was now splattered on the floor around the corpse. Where there should have been a face, was a large gaping hole with grey brain-matter spilling out, like someone mixed too much ketchup with rotten scrambled eggs.

In its hands there was a shotgun.

"Oh god," said Janice.

"Everything okay?" asked Gary, coming over.

She didn't say anything and just motioned to behind the counter. Gary looked and then jerked back.

"Whoa, well that fucker's dead alright," he said. "Let's just grab what we need and get out of here."

He reached carefully over the counter and grabbed a bunch of plastic bags. He gave some of them to Janice and the two got to work looting.

"Car's gassed up," said Benny stepping into the store. "How's it going in here?"

"We got one really fucked-up dead guy behind the counter," said Gary.

"Let's just get our shit and get out of here," said Janice. "This place is giving me the creeps."

Soon the DeLorean was loaded up with jerky, candy, chips, soda, beer, jumper-cables, oil, water, cigarettes, and other random odds and ends they could grab.

On the last trip of loading up, Benny and Janice were sorting the supplies out at the car, while Gary was grabbing a last couple beers. He carried two six-packs out of the store when three shapes appeared in the doorway. Two men and a woman blocked his path. Wires and various electronic equipment were jammed into the grey flesh of their arms and face. The woman zombie had replaced all her teeth with computer chips.

"Hey, guys," shouted Gary.

He stumbled back and the three Zombie Borg walked into the store. One male zombie had staplers jammed into his face where his eyes should have been. The other was missing its left hand and a blender had been jammed into the gory stump.

"We are the Borg. We will add your biological and technological distinctiveness to our own," they said in unison.

"Guys," Gary yelled. "I could use a little help here."

Gary backed up as the three Zombie Borg moved closer to him.

"Holy shit," said Benny from the doorway.

He and Janice came inside.

"Nice of you guys to show up," said Gary, now in the back corner of the store. "I could use a little help."

One of the male Zombie Borgs turned to face Benny and Janice.

"We are the Borg," they said. The male Zombie Borg raised its arm and the blender whirled.

Janice ran behind the counter. She looked down at the bloody body clutching the shotgun and paused. She looked back at the advancing monsters and tore the gun from the dead hands.

She came around counter and pumped the weapon. The zombie raised its arms and whirled the blender at her while she raised the gun.

Blam!

The shot took the head off not just the Zombie Borg advancing on her but also the one standing behind it. Their heads popped and splattered blood and gore over Gary. The neck stumps spurted blood and the bodies slumped to the ground.

The third Zombie Borg, the woman with the computer chips for teeth turned to her. "We are the—"

Benny grabbed the fire extinguisher off the wall and slammed it into the thing's head. The Zombie Borg dropped to its knees and its head wobbled around. Benny brought back the extinguisher and swung it forward. The back of the Zombie Borg's skull caved in. Its eyes popped out along with a stream of gore from the sockets. It fell face first to the ground.

"Let's go," said Benny and he rushed for the door. Gary ran behind brandishing a magazine rack and Janice with the shotgun.

Four more Zombie Borg milled around the DeLorean. They were banging at the windows while Squishy bounced around inside hissing.

Janice walked up behind one of them and fired off another blast into the back of the monster's head. Benny swung the extinguisher and dropped the second. Gary ran

50

forward with the magazine rack out to push back the other two. The corpses stumbled back and fell over each other.

"Get in," shouted Benny as he swung open the door. Janice jumped in while Gary hit the fallen Zombie Borg again with the magazine rack.

"We are the Borg," they said.

"You are an asshole," Gary said and spit on them.

He got into the car and they drove off in the direction of the highway, fully stocked with gas, supplies, and food.

In the parking lot, the two Zombie Borg they left alive struggled to get back to their feet.

"We are the Borg."

They began to stumble in the direction of the DeLorean—West.

Five more Zombie Borg walked out of the tall corn fields surrounding the gas station.

"We will add your biological and technological distinctiveness to our own."

Another dozen Zombie Borg shuffled across the road. Then more and more of the walking dead swarmed out of the fields. Their bodies were torn from violent death and mutilated with wires, electronic parts, and vacuum cleaner tubes. They all headed in the same direction.

"Resistance is futile."

8
THE CULT OF KIRK

The plaque was simple and cheap, little more than a rock with a flat metal slab on top. Etched in its surface was:

Riverside, Iowa
Future Birthplace of
Captain James. T. Kirk
March 22, 2228

Gary stood in front of it, posing with an exaggerated smile and giving the Vulcan salute. Benny tapped Gary's phone and took a picture. Gary ran over and looked at the screen with glee.

"Sweet," he said taking back the phone. He tapped it a few times. "It's just my luck. I finally make it here and I can't upload to Facebook."

"So why did we go out of our way to come here?" asked Janice as she looked around the town. She held the shotgun ready.

"She has a point," said Benny. He spun around scanning the town. "This is a pretty boring monument. At least there's some cars around."

"Oh, come on," said Gary. "Embrace the moment. Soak up the glory of Kirk. This is an offer to our journey." He jumped up, "I'm going to get a picture of Squishy with the plaque."

Gary picked up the wheezing cat and set her down next to the rock.

"This feels weird," said Janice.

"Smile, Squishy," Gary said while taking a picture.

Squishy burped.

"Gary, will you focus," said Janice.

Gary sighed and turned around. "OK, fine. What is it?"

"Where is everybody?" she asked.

"They're all dead."

"OK, fine. Then what killed them?"

"Ummm . . . huh." Gary looked around the picturesque small town. The small houses and local shops looked like a set from *It's A Wonderful Life*. There were several cars on the street but they were parked, not haphazardly abandoned or wrecked like what had been the standard on their trip.

"It is a little spooky," said Gary.

"Nothing's broken or smashed up," said Benny.

"There's just no people," said Janice.

"I'd wager something bad still happened here," said Benny.

Then they came out from every alleyway and from behind every building—dozens of people from every direction. They all wore the same white full body robes. Their hoods up and heads down, obscuring their faces. All that was visible was their feet and they all wore the same style of bright-red sneaker.

Benny, Gary, and Janice huddled closer together and spun around. Janice had the gun pointed out but there were so many of them. There were at least a hundred and they were completely surrounded.

"Well, fuck," said Gary.

The robed figures parted and one person walked up to them. Unlike all the others, his garment was gold.

"Welcome travelers. Welcome to Riverside," said the man as he flipped back his golden hood. He was middle-aged with the beginning of peppered hair. He smiled and his eyes shone with kindness.

"Ummm. . . .Hi," said Benny.

The other figures lifted their heads and dropped their hoods. There were men and women, young and old. The faces looked like the demographic of a normal small town in the middle of Indiana, their faces glowed with kindness and curiosity.

"There's really no need for that," said David pointing to Janice. She was holding the shotgun raised and ready.

She looked at Benny and he nodded. She lowered the gun.

"I'm David Marcus," said the man holding out his hand.

They all shook it and introduced themselves.

"So what brings you to our town? On foot no less."

"Our car broke down about two miles down the road, just off the highway," said Benny. "We walked here."

"We're here to pay our respects," said Gary pointing to plaque.

"Wonderful," said David. "I should have known from your uniforms. There's not much else our town is known for."

"Is there anyone that could help us with our car?" asked Janice.

"Of course," said David. "But you look like you had quite the journey and we're just about to sit down for dinner. Come join us as our guests."

David outstretched his arms and gave them a big smile. His teeth flawlessly white and perfectly straight.

"What do you think?" said Janice.

"It would be nice to have a home-cooked meal," said Benny.

"Wonderful," said David.

***

They sat in the community center along with all the robed townspeople. Three long tables filled the hall. Each seated about thirty and almost every seat was filled. Benny, Gary, and Janice sat at the head of the center table with the gold-robed David seated next to them.

Everyone ate bowls of a hearty meat stew. Squishy was underneath the table snorting and lapping from her own dish.

"So you're from Pennsylvania," said David taking another spoonful of stew.

"Yeah," replied Benny, "we're all from Stewartstown.

It's in south central P.A., along the Maryland border. But . . . it's not there anymore."

"So what brings you out this way?"

"We're on a mission to save Captain Kirk," said Gary jumping into the conversation.

"Kirk," grinned David. "I knew from your uniforms that you were followers."

"Followers?" asked Janice.

"Followers of the great captain, our admiral of all things. We live to serve Kirk."

"So . . . it's like a religion?" asked Janice.

"It is our belief. We live by his lessons."

Gary grinned and chewed on a hunk of meat. "Sounds like something I could get behind." He chewed loudly and looked around the room. "So everyone here is part of your . . . belief?"

"Yes, we are all followers."

"Well, we thank you for your hospitality," said Benny. "Like I said before, our car is broken down on the edge of your town. We'd appreciate it if there's a mechanic you could direct us to."

"Of course we can but there is no need to continue your journey."

"And why is that?" asked Benny.

"Because Kirk is here."

They looked at each other, surprised. Even Squishy sensed the change in mood and stopped lapping.

"He's here?" asked Gary.

"Of course. It's the end of the world. Where else would he go but his hometown? In times of peril we all want to go home."

They all looked around the room but didn't see Shatner anywhere amongst the townspeople.

"Where is he?"

"Kirk stays to himself. We bring him food and women and he bestows upon us his blessings."

"Can . . . can we see him?"

"Of course. But not now. The hour is turning late and

you must be tired. You've come a long way. Spend the night and rest."

"But when can we see him?" pushed Gary.

David smiled. "We can talk about it in the morning."

"Could someone give us a lift to our car so we can grab a few things?" asked Benny.

"It will be better to wait until daylight. The roads aren't . . . safe to be on at night," said David. "But I insist, Meredith will show you to your rooms and everything will be sorted out in the morning."

***

"Dude, this is all fucking wrong," said Gary while pacing around the narrow room. He crouched down in front of the old television again and tried working the knobs. He slammed the side of the box and mumbled under his breath.

"Will you calm down with that TV," said Benny.

After the dinner they were led to a house nearby the community center. Benny and Gary were shown to a room to share and Janice was given her own.

"I'm not liking this either," said Benny. He held up the clothes that were laid out on the two beds for them to change into—the same white robes everyone was wearing. And a pair of red sneakers for each of them.

The door to their room burst open and Janice stormed in. She shut the door behind and threw down another white robe and pair of red sneakers.

"I'm not wearing that and there's something really wrong here," she said.

"Yeah, that's what I was just saying," said Gary. "And David Marcus? That's the name of Kirk's son from the movies."

Benny was looking out the window of the room but he didn't see anything suspicious. "He seemed pretty serious that Shatner was here."

"I don't believe it," said Janice.

"Neither do I," said Benny.

"I really don't want to wait 'til morning to find out," said Gary sitting down on the bed.

"Yeah, he got really weird about that there," said Janice.

"He didn't want us to see Shatner. He didn't want us to go back to our car," thought Benny out loud. "He just wanted us to spend the night here."

"Dude, I've seen enough horror movies to know where this is going," said Gary.

"Alright, so we just dash?" said Janice.

"But they worship Kirk and said he was here," said Gary. "They seem pretty serious about that."

"So who do they have here?" asked Janice.

"Fuck if I know," said Gary. "But I'd really like to find out."

"But where would we even begin," said Janice.

"I think I might know," said Benny looking out the room's window.

It was a normal small town street with shops, a post office, and a bar. At the end of the street was the town's church. Someone had taken the cross down from the steeple and had replaced it with a homemade wooden Star Trek insignia.

9
GARY MITCHELL'S STORY

Gary tied off his arm, just above the bicep, with shoelaces he bought from the convenience store down the street. The store clerk gave him a dirty look as he pointed to them in the glass case behind the counter, but fuck that guy.

He tapped the syringe and pushed it up a little, making sure there were no bubbles, and lined up the needle with the large black and blue bruise on his forearm. In the center of the angry bruise was an open wound of scabs and black pus. A perfect bull's eye.

The needle point slid easily into the open wound and there was a stinging pain in his arm. He pushed down on the syringe and the drugs flowed into his veins.

He was immediately hit with the euphoria and roughly jerked the needle out. Gary flopped back on the stain and tore up couch.

"Yo, dude you done?"

"Uh-huh," Gary slurred and passed the syringe to the next person.

"It's good shit isn't it?" said a voice from somewhere in the haze.

"Oh, yeah," said Gary. This was some strong stuff. He was finding it hard to hold his head up.

"Are, you okay dude?" someone asked.

Gary wanted to say he was but he couldn't seem to get his tongue to work anymore. He tried to sit up to get a glass of water but his body didn't want to do what he told it to. He rolled off the couch and tumbled to the dirty wooden floor.

"Yo, I don't think this guy's doing so good."

Gary wanted to tell them he was fine but nothing was working and everything was getting very blurry.

His hand was limp on the floor in front of his face and a

cockroach ran across it.

Need to lay more traps, Gary thought and then everything went black.

***

"You know you're lucky to be alive."

Gary didn't respond. He scratched at the bandages around his wrists.

The doctor flipped through his file. "Judging from the infections and scars, you've been abusing the shit out of yourself for years. We got you prescribed to antibiotics. That should clear it up."

Gary just continued to stare off.

"Maybe some time with family and a change of scenery will do you some good."

***

"You know you're a real fuck-up," said Gary's dad as he cracked open another PBR.

Gary just stared down.

"God damn it son. Heroin, *really?* Thank god your mom ain't around to see this."

He looked at his son with mean, disappointed eyes.

"I'd fixed up the basement for you. Not like you're going to say thanks. Just stay out of my way."

And Gary did stay out of his father's way. His dad had a day job as a butcher at the local supermarket where he worked shifts from six in the morning to six in the evening.

Gary slept all day and stayed up all night. He managed to get a cheap TV from a pawnshop down the street and would just tune into whatever syndication had for him. It was all meaningless dreck but every night at three a.m. *Star Trek* came on. He had never watched it before. He had nothing against *Star Trek* but he had just never seen it.

Watching the adventures of Kirk, Spock, and McCoy took him away every night. There was something about the adventures of the USS Enterprise which made him feel hope and happiness—even though it was just a television show.

Soon the rest of the shows held little interest to him and he stopped watching them. He kept up with *Star Trek* but watched little else. The spin-offs were OK but they were nothing like the original series.

While he waited for *Star Trek* to come on he would play around at his computer. Since he was a little kid he had played around with writing. Nothing much, just little stories to amuse himself.

Now, a broken young adult, he started to tell himself stories again. He started with shorts about Kirk and Spock and untold adventures they had. And then he began to write scripts. Episodes about McCoy having to solve the problem of the tribble-Borg, of Spock getting hooked on meth after trying it for logical reasons, and of Kirk battling the Gorn once again (Gary hadn't seen the animated series).

He would print out the scripts and send them to an address he found off the official Star Trek website but he never received a response.

***

It took a while but eventually the sores on his arms cleared up and he was bored of spending so much time in that dark basement. He wanted to go out during the day and see some sunlight again. He went for short walks around town and on one such stroll came across Brave Nerd World. In the display windows were various comic books and action figures.

He went inside and walked in a daze amongst the aisles. Comic books, action figures, and various other collectibles filled every available space. Soon he came across a display of Star Trek toys. There were figures of all the crew members, clip-on insignias, and—what caught Gary's eye—a phaser replica. It was just a cheap plastic kids toy but it made a different sound depending on the setting (all authentic to the television series) and looked fucking awesome.

He took it up to the counter and was paying for it when

someone else in the store stopped to talk.

"Nice phaser. You into Trek?"

Gary turned. The person speaking to him was another guy, about his age. Another bland nerd, but for the satchel around his side holding a fat cat.

***

"Dude, haven't seen you for a while."

Gary turned around and there was Splinter. Gary hadn't seen him since the old days.

"Yeah," said Gary. "I've been keeping to myself, mostly."

"I heard you had a real bad trip back there."

"Yeah, but I've been doing better."

Gary took a sip of his beer and looked around the house nervously. It was an old, barely holding together, punk house with show flyers and political posters plastered all over the walls. The living room had been emptied out for bands to play but right now it was in-between acts. Everyone was just milling about drinking beer and chatting. He was hoping to meet some new people this evening, not see Splinter.

"Good to hear man, good to hear. So, you still usin'?"

Gary looked him in the eyes. It was obvious Splinter was still on the shit. His short, skinny body was wrapped in an oversized Member's Only jacket and it had to be at least ninety degrees in the house. His face was dotted with open meth sores and he had shaved off his eyebrows since they last saw each other. In their place he had "FUCK" and "YOU" tattooed in their place.

"Nah, I haven't been," replied Gary.

"Ah, that's too bad. But yo, dude, it's so exciting to see you again. Some boys and me are getting lit upstairs. Whatta say? Just a little for old time's sake."

Gary wanted to say "no" right away but he couldn't. He started to salivate. He hadn't really felt tempted since his time in the hospital but he hadn't really had an opportunity since then either.

"Sure," he spoke before he knew what he was doing.

61

"Why the fuck not? Just a little."

"That's the fuckin' spirit," Splinter said and slapped him on the back.

He led Gary through the house and up the creaky stairs. There was a small hallway with five doors. Splinter went to the furthest door and knocked.

"Yo, it's me."

"Come in," someone shouted from inside.

Splinter opened the door and gave a crocked-tooth grin to Gary.

It was a small room with a bare mattress with a blanket on top. In the corner was a wooden table with an old small TV and a PS1 hooked up. There were five people sitting around the corners of the room. All punks with matted long hair and cheap tattoos. In the center of the floor was a pile of syringes, twine, metal spoons, and small gram baggies of white powder.

"You ready to do this?" asked Splinter as he dropped to his knees and began prepping the supplies.

"Uh, yeah," said Gary sitting down next to him. He looked around at the other people in the room but they were all strung out on their own trip and paid him no mind.

"So what's with this shit I hear about you gettin' into all this nerd shit? And you're becoming a magician or something?" asked Splinter as he opened one of the plastic bags.

"*Magic: the Gathering*. It's a card game. I've been playing it with some friends."

"A card game? Like Poke-e-man, that's kinda whack."

"It's a lot of fun."

"I'll take your word for it," said Splinter. He turned and held out a syringe to Gary. "But so's this shit."

There were still little scars on Gary's arms, making finding the right spot so easy.

And then he drifted away. He leaned back against the peeling-paint covered wall and shut his eyes.

"See," said Splinter. "I told you it was fun."

"I already fucking knew that."

***

"Gary . . . Gary . . . wake up."

"Huh."

"You . . . must . . . wake up."

Gary sat up, his back aching, and rubbed his eyes. His head hurt.

"Where am I," he mumbled as the blurriness left his vision.

He was still in the same room but everyone else was gone. The table had been moved while he was passed out and the television on top had been turned on. It was the original series *Star Trek.* The screen was showing a shot of the bridge, empty but for Kirk sitting in the captain's chair and staring straight at the screen.

"Gary," said Kirk. "Are you . . . with me?"

"What?"

"Good . . . dear god . . . man . . . look at yourself . . . what . . . are . . . you doing?"

Gary looked down at his arm and the syringe was still stuck in his vein. A thin trickle of dried blood ran down his skin.

"I . . . I'm not sure," said Gary.

"You're going . . . to . . . kill yourself."

"Fuck," said Gary rolling his eyes. Even Captain Kirk was going to give him some moralistic bullshit.

"Now . . . I'm not going . . . to . . . feed you . . . some moralistic bullshit."

Gary peaked up.

"I . . . need you, Gary," continued Kirk. "And I'll need . . . you . . . to stay sharp."

"What do you need me to do, Captain?"

"Not . . . right now . . . but you need . . . to . . . get out of here."

***

Gary sat up. The sun streaming in through the window hurt his eyes. He was still in the punk house. The table and TV were back in the corner like the night before. The room was empty except for Splinter, leaning up against the wall next to him.

Gary looked down and saw that the syringe was still stuck in his arm. He carefully pulled it out and a little spurt of blood left his vein.

"Yo, Splinter. Wake up," said Gary while he shook Splinter's shoulders.

Splinter fell forward and hit the floor with a *THUD*. His head was tilted at an awkward angle. His blank, glassy eyes stared straight at Gary. Dead.

"Oh Splinter. Fucking idiot," he said and got to his feet.

He left the room and walked down the stairs. The show was long over but there were a few scattered punks sleeping on the floor. Gary left the house and shut the door behind.

***

It was three a.m. and channel six always showed original series reruns at this time. Gary sat on the edge of his bed while the opening theme played.

The credits rolled and there was Captain Kirk sitting on the bridge looking right at Gary.

"What's up?" asked Gary.

"Oh . . . same old . . . same old," said Kirk. "I have . . . a . . . cameo in the . . . new . . . *Star Trek* movie."

"Yeah, I saw that on Twitter. I don't know why you're validating these remakes, but whatever. I'll still go see it. Oh, did you get my package?"

"Yes . . . I did."

"And what'd you think of the script?"

"It was . . . good . . . but does there need to be . . . so . . . many . . . gay sex scenes?"

"Yeah, I took some artistic license. Any other feedback?"

"I'll . . . send some . . . later."

"Cool, cool." Gary said. "Hey, remember when we first met in that house?"

Kirk nodded.

"You said you'd need me. What did you mean? What do you need me for?"

Kirk smiled and the camera zoomed in for a close-up. "Oh . . . you'll know . . . when . . . it's time."

10
WILL THE REAL CAPTAIN KIRK PLEASE STAND UP?

"Alright, let's do this," said Benny.

They walked up the steps of the church, Benny, Gary, and Janice all in a line. Squishy was in her bag and Janice had the shotgun.

It appeared that someone had torn down the cross and replaced it with a homemade Star Fleet insignia. It was made of plywood and crudely hammered together.

Benny opened the door and they stepped in. Candles flickered along the edges and the pews had been torn out to make one large open space. There were cheap cardboard sets, like one would see in a community theater production sprawled through the room.

"What have they been doing in here?" asked Benny.

"Looks like they were making fan films," replied Janice with her gun pointed out and ready for any attack. "Dude," said Gary walking over to a fake rocky arch. "It's the Guardian of Forever."

"That looks like Cyrano Jones' Bar."

"Check out the windows," said Janice.

Benny and Gary looked up at the stained-glass windows that once showed scenes of Jesus' life. They had all been replaced with murals of the adventures and triumphs of the Captain of the USS Enterprise. Kirk fighting the Gorn, Kirk in a fistfight with Khan, and Kirk from that episode where he taught that planet what sex was.

"Jesus," said Janice. "These people make you look normal, Gary."

At the front of the room there was a sudden snort and loud snore.

"Someone's here," said Benny.

They carefully crept through the dark church. At the front

of the room was a small stage, where the altar should be, but instead there was a throne and a person slumped down in it. The flickering candles obscured the figure in shadows.

As they got closer they could see that the throne was made of bones. Long femurs made the base and the back was spines woven together. The top was decorated with a row of skulls. Unlike the sets, these did not look like cheap props.

The figure sitting on top snored loudly.

Gary was the first to speak up.

"Ummm . . . Hello?"

The figure snorted and sat up. He was wearing the original series uniform. The top part was gold for command. His hair was cut to resemble Kirk but . . .

The three exchanged a curious look.

"Isn't that Chris Pine?" said Janice

He shook the sleep from his head and looked down at the four of them. They stared at each other for a minute and then Chris Pine spoke.

"Why do you come before the Kirk?"

"You ain't no fucking Kirk," said Gary.

Pine cocked his head, "I am the Kirk."

"You're a Kirk but you're not *the* Kirk."

Pine leaned forward and gripped the arm rests of the throne. "*I am the Kirk.*"

There was the sound of doors bursting open from behind the altar and more cultists came storming in. The trio surrounded. The townspeople were armed with hammers, pipes, scythes, and butcher knives.

"Oh, this is not good," said Janice while raising the shotgun higher.

They poured in and filled the church, standing several rows thick. These were not the same happy and curious townspeople they saw earlier in the evening. Their faces now looked crazy with bloodlust and hunger. A small man with a screwdriver was licking his lips at them.

"They said I am not the Kirk," said Chris Pine as he stood up from the throne and walked to the edge of the small stage. "Who are these doubters?"

The townspeople parted and the town leader in the gold robe came walking through. He approached them and dropped his hood. Squishy hissed from her bag.

"Newcomers," said David to Pine. He turned and faced them. "I thought we had agreed we were to talk about Kirk sometime later?" He smiled daggers.

Benny locked eyes with him and then turned to Chris Pine. Pine was standing at the edge of the stage and had his chest puffed out while looking them over, like a predator.

"It is of no concern. You see, there's one more thing you should know about us . . . we eat people."

"What?" asked Benny.

"You're a fucking Kirk-based cult. Why would you be eating people?" said Gary. "If you were a proper Kirk-based cult you'd be having orgies all the time and denouncing other people's Gods."

"We do that too," replied David.

He motioned to one of the cult members. A massive man of almost seven feet tall came out of the crowd and up to Janice.

"Would you be so kind as to give him your firearm? I don't believe you'll find it can save you now."

"What if I just shot you instead?" said Janice.

"You could do that," said David. "But how many shots do you think you can get off before we'd overtake you."

Janice looked around at the dozens of hungry and crazy eyes looking back at her.

"Give them the gun," whispered Benny.

"What?" said Janice.

"We fight now we're dead," he said. "Give them the gun and we might have a chance."

Her eyes flicked around the room again. She nodded at Gary and then held out the shotgun. The tall man snatched it from her hands and stepped back to the crowd, pointing the gun at them.

"Wonderful, now the next pressing issue is you three. This was to wait until morning but now is just as good of a time. It's good you came along. We've been running low on nonbelievers and the three of you are quite vital nutrients at this time."

Squishy hissed.

"And the cat too. We'll eat the cat. Take them."

The cultists came at them from every direction.

***

"Move," said the cultist, pushing Gary.

He stumbled forward and turned back. "What the fuck do you think I'm doing?"

Gary turned to Benny. "These guys are real assholes. I don't think I want to join their religion anymore."

"Shut up," shouted the cultist and pushed Gary again.

Benny, Gary, and Janice were being led down the street by the group of cultists from the church. Once they got outside, they lit up thick torches, like you'd see in those old Universal horror movies. In the flickering light, they could see there were at least a hundred cultists.

Their hands were bound behind their backs with thick rope and they were pushed forward.

"*Aaarrrwww!*"

"Hey," shouted Benny. "Careful with my cat."

They had taken Squishy from Benny's satchel and tied her paws to a broomstick. Two cultists carried each end of the stick and she dangled upside down like a hunted-down wild pig. She glared at the cultists carrying her and wheezed louder than normal.

The cultists talked amongst themselves like they were out for an evening stroll. There was almost a jovial sense to the air—it didn't feel like a death march.

They came to the main intersection of town in front of city hall and it didn't look like Bedford Falls anymore. A huge bonfire filled the street. Drums beat from somewhere within the immense crowd and cultists danced around the fire in pagan-like fervor.

They were led to the left side of the fire and pushed down to their knees. They were dozens of feet away but the heat was still intense.

Squishy was tossed to the ground in front of them.

"*Aaarrww!*"

Most of the cultists had already joined the crowd but a few stayed behind to keep guard.

"So how do you think we're going to get out of this one?" said Gary.

"I'm . . . I'm not so sure we are," said Janice.

Now that they were closer to the fire, they could see that the people dancing around the fire were all women. Their skin had been dyed green and they wildly gyrated their hips and stared with lust at the surrounding crowd.

"I don't think you're looking at this situation properly," said Gary.

"And how do you see this?" said Janice.

In front of the city hall there was a large, flat wooden platform. David Marcus stood atop it and looked out over the assembling crowd with pleasure on his face.

"OK, we're a small group of adventurers on a specific mission. We encounter a strange new group of people, and dining with them, we become suspicious. After sneaking around when and where we're not supposed to be, we discover a horrible secret and are captured. What does that sound like to you?"

Janice shook her head exasperated. "That we're fucked?"

Gary rolled his eyes. "No. It's the plot line of half of the episodes of the original series. We're going to make it out of this just fine."

"Jesus Christ," shouted Janice. "This isn't a fucking TV show."

Gary smiled. "Just you wait. We'll get out of this."

Squishy thrashed against her restraints and whined. She rolled over so she was facing Benny. She looked up with big scared eyes. She wheezed and her red uniform quickly rose and fell.

"It's okay," said Benny softly. "It's going to be okay."

David moved to the end of the stage and raised his hand. The drums stopped and a hush went over the crowd. All the cultists turned their attention to him.

"Iowa," he yelled.

"*The final frontier,*" the cultists replied in unison. The huge number of people shouting the same words seemed to make the ground shake.

"These are the adventures," he said.

"*Of the town Riverside,*" the cultists boomed.

"Its never ending mission."

"*To survive.*"

"By any means necessary."

"*To put ourselves before any outsider.*"

"To boldly go."

"*However far we must.*"

The crowd exploded in cheers and a group of fifty women moved into five orderly rows on the far side of the fire and they began to sing.

"*Ahhh, ahhh, ahhh-ah-ah-ah-ah-ahn.*"

"Is that—?" said Janice.

"Yep," said Gary interrupting her. "It's the theme to *Star Trek.*"

The crowd parted and then Chris Pine came through. He was still seated on his throne which was now attached to two long boards. Each end was supported by a cultist and they carried him through the crowd. Pine waved as the cultists cheered.

He was taken to the stage and, with the aid of several other waiting cultists, his throne was hoisted up. He looked out over the adoring crowd like a smug king. David stood next to him beaming like a kid on Christmas morning.

Pine then waved his hand, the crowd went silent, and the singing stopped.

David moved to the front of the stage again. "As is our way, and has always been, and always will be, we must open tonight's service with a sacrifice to the great and all-mighty Kirk."

"God, God, no!" screamed a woman from somewhere in the back of the crowd.

The large cultist dragged a naked woman out to the front of the bonfire. She was pulled by long chains attached to metal shackles around her legs. Her hands were tied behind her back and she thrashed her body around.

"Please, please," she pleaded through tears.

Another pair of cultists pushed over what looked like wood scaffolding on wheels. At the bottom of the contraption was a wooden pole. They attached her shackles to the pole and turned a wheel on the side of the device. As the wheel turned, the wooden pole rose, and after a few turns of the wheel, she was hanging in the air upside-down.

"No, no. Don't do this," she screamed.

Another cultist placed a wooden basin beneath her head. He drew out a long, serrated knife and held it over the woman. The blade was pointed at her bare crotch.

"No, no," she screamed and thrashed around. The cultist reached out with his other hand to hold her steady.

He looked back at Pine.

Pine nodded and said, "Make it so."

The knife plunged down into her vagina and the cultist grabbed the handle with both hands and dropped to his knees, ripping down the blade.

"*AAAAAAHHHH—*"

Her scream lasted for just a moment before her body flipped open from groin to sternum. Her organs, intestines, and blood poured out over her head and into the basin beneath.

The body swayed on the shackles and the crowd roared with approval.

"My god," said Benny.

"That's terrible," said Janice.

"He didn't even get it right," said Gary.

Benny and Janice looked at him.

"Picard says 'make it so,'" said Gary. "Not Kirk."

"Now is not the time," hissed Janice.

"It's a relevant issue."

"Hush," said Benny. "He's going to talk again."

David waved his arms and the crowd went silent again.

"Brothers and Sisters," he said. "I apologized for having to rouse you at such a late hour but there is an issue that requires our community's attention. Tonight, outsiders came to town."

"*Ohhhhhh,*" went the crowd.

The woman was lowered off the rack and the shackles were undone from her feet. Her corpse was slung into a wheelbarrow and hauled away.

"And they brought with them the threat of violence," continued David. He held up Janice's shotgun.

"*Booooo,*" went the crowd.

"This is a peaceful town. We follow the teachings of Kirk and firearms have no place here."

David tossed the shotgun from the platform into the bonfire and the crowd cheered.

"As is our way, they must be punished." David looked over at Benny, Gary, and Janice and smiled but there was no friendship, only malice and hunger. "The sentence is—"

The crowd hushed.

"Death!"

The crowd roared with approval.

"May your trespass and aggression fill our bellies," said David looking right at them.

Cultists moved in and lifted them to their feet, pushing them in the direction of the slaughter apparatus. Two cultists picked up Squishy and she hissed.

They struggled, but with their hands tied, they were easily shoved over to the machine and forced to their knees again.

"Come on," mumbled Gary looking around.

"Janice," said Benny.

Benny could see she was starting to cry.

"Come on," mumbled Gary.

In all the commotion of the crowd, the screams weren't immediately obvious. They blended in with the general party/ritual sacrifice atmosphere. But when the screams began to outnumber the cheers, the crowd began to take notice and the mood changed.

"We are the Borg," came from every direction.

The crowd around the bonfire broke apart and people

began to scatter and scream.

Benny, Gary, and Janice looked around. They didn't see anything at first but then the familiar stagger and grey dead flesh of the Zombie Borg staggered into view.

They came from every direction. Every man, woman, and child of Riverside, Iowa was stuck in a death trap as the drones poured in.

The would-be-executioner was caught between two Zombie Borg that looked like they raided the same vacuum cleaner. They each grabbed an arm and pulled. The man shrieked and then there was a sound like fabric tearing and both arms wrenched free of the sockets. Blood sprayed from the wounds turning the man's robe deep crimson and he fell to the ground.

"Stay down," shouted Gary lying on the ground. "If they don't think we're a threat, they'll leave us alone."

"You can't be—" started Janice.

"Just get down," yelled Gary.

Janice and Benny did as he said, and two Zombie Borg shambled past them into the chaos.

"See," said Gary watching them go.

"They're fucking brain dead," said Janice. "They didn't see us."

Benny struggled against his ropes. "We need to get out of these."

"I can't budge mine," said Janice.

"Me neither," said Gary.

"Fuck," shouted Benny.

"Here," he said and turned his back to Janice. "See if you can work on my knots and I'll see if I can get yours."

She backed against them and their fingers fumbled at the ropes but their hands were too restrained.

"I can't get a grip," she said.

"Me neither."

Gary looked around. The bonfire roared and illuminated a massacre. The ground became wet with blood. While many of the cultists were armed with simple weapons, they were totally unprepared for the assault.

A Zombie Borg with a lawnmower sticking out of his head pushed a little girl to the ground. It climbed on top of her and pushed in her eyes with its thumbs. It stood up and turned around.

"Bet . . . you . . . didn't expect to see me," said Captain Kirk.

A small portable television was lodged in the Zombie Borg's chest. The screen faced out and was turned on. Captain Kirk smiled out of it at Gary.

"Well about fucking time," said Gary.

The Zombie Borg began to move toward him.

"I . . . don't think . . . I need . . . to . . . tell you . . . you must . . . get free."

"Well duh."

"We are the Borg," said the corpse.

"But how the hell am I going to do that?" said Benny.

"I . . . don't know . . . but it would be . . . helpful . . . if you had . . . something sharp . . . something to cut . . . the ropes."

Right then, a cultist with a lead pipe rushed up and bashed the monster in the chest, shattering the screen. The Zombie Borg stumbled back and the cultist raised the pipe over his head and brought it down hard, crushing the monster's skull. It twitched and crumbled to the ground and the cultist rushed off into the battle.

Gary saw the jagged glass of the shattered television screen and crawled over to the fallen zombie. He felt for the sharp glass with his fingers.

Ow! His finger stung as it was cut. *Found it.* He began to saw at the rope.

"Janice," said Benny.

She looked up at him.

"I really didn't see it going down like this," he said.

She struggled against the ropes and then relaxed. "I don't think any of us did."

"No I mean, there's something I want to say."

Gary sawed at the ropes and another Zombie Borg came lurching at him.

"Resistance is futile," it said as it fell on top of Gary. He braced his legs against it and kicked back. The corpse fell backwards and Gary's ropes snapped against the glass.

"What is it?" said Janice.

"I wanted you to know—"

"Hey, hey," said Gary running over with his hands free. He went behind Janice and began to undo her restraints. "Hope I didn't keep you waiting."

Janice was free and she rubbed her wrists.

"What was that?" she asked, as Gary undid Benny.

"It can wait," said Benny.

He turned to where Squishy had been dropped but she was gone. There was just the broomstick and a pile of shredded rope.

"Where's Squishy?" said Benny.

They looked around at the battle between cultists and Zombie Borg.

"I think that's her," said Janice pointing.

Across the fight was a cultist staggering through the commotion. He was beating at his head—which seemed to be enveloped in white and brown fur.

They ran over, dodging roaming zombies and fleeing cultists.

The man staggered around screaming, "My eyes! My eyes!" while Squishy slashed again and again.

"The bitch is tearing him apart," marveled Gary.

"Squishy," shouted Benny.

She ignored him. The cultist screamed and thrashed around trying to shake the cat free. He tripped over his own feet and tumbled to the ground. Squishy squealed and clawed even more frantically.

Benny looked around nervously, "Squishy!" He darted forward, grabbed her, and pulled. She didn't want to let go. Benny yanked harder and heard a ripping sound. The cultist screamed as Squishy came free.

Deep, bleeding cuts covered the man's face. His eye sockets were just two ruined messes of white jelly and red pulp. He screamed and Squishy hissed.

Benny put Squishy in his satchel, the cultists had never taken it away.

"Good Squishy," said Gary and patted her on the head. She purred.

"Come on," said Benny, he pointed down a street away from the battle.

They ran about two blocks until they saw a white van in the alleyway. Next to the driver's side door, a mangled corpse was still clutching a set of keys.

Gary ran up to the body and pulled the keys from its hand.

"You know," he said. "We've been really fucking lucky with this."

He unlocked the van and they all got into the front seats.

Gary turned to Janice, "what did I tell you about us getting out of here?"

"Well it's about time," said a voice from behind them.

They all screamed and spun around to see Chris Pine sitting on the floor of the van.

"So are we fucking going??" he asked.

Gary shrugged. "The man's got a point."

He backed the van out of the alley and turned it to head out of the town. They drove down the street and passed people having their throats and organs torn out and then appliances and wires shoved into their body.

Then Gary stopped the van.

"What the fuck are you doing?" asked Janice.

He took off his seat belt and climbed out of the driver's seat into the back of the van.

"Benny, take the wheel."

Benny just looked back at Gary.

"Dude, do it!"

Benny slid over, started the van back up, and they started moving again down the road.

Gary grinned at Christ Pine. "Tell J. J. I'll see him in hell."

"Uhhhh . . ."

Gary opened the back doors of the van, grabbed Pine by the collar of his shirt, and threw him out. He tumbled out and landed hard on the street. Gary could hear the thump as they moved away.

Pine rolled around in pain from the fall as six Zombie Borg descended upon him. They pulled at his limbs and dug into his flesh.

"Gary," shouted Janice. "What the hell?"

Gary ignored her and flipped off the screaming, thrashing body of Chris Pine as they drove away. One of the Zombie Borg wrenched free his right arm and shambled off with the prize.

"Fuck you Pine. Fuck you and the remakes."

PART 2

WHITE POWER KLINGON BIKERS FROM HELL

11
JANICE CHAPEL'S STORY

Janice was a geek. She collected *Magic: the Gathering* cards, played SNES RPGs, owned a complete collection of collectible Lego minfigs, and could out trivia anyone at Marvel comics and *Babylon 5*.

But she was alone. All the guys she met in the nerd scene were nerds of the worst degree. Either they constantly doubted her knowledge or after a few dates "barefoot in the kitchen" jokes came out.

That's why she was so happy to meet Vash. He ordered a double espresso at the coffee shop where she worked. He was tall and well dressed and his smile just melted her. When he asked for her number and if she wanted to get a drink, there was no way she could say no.

On that date she learned that he was an investment banker. His passion was numbers and following the market. It's what he went to school for and had been doing for most of his life. She didn't care that she found his career boring as shit—he had a real passion for something.

But when she told him what her passions were he made a funny face.

"Well, nobody's perfect."

***

They kept seeing each other and their relationship grew. He took her out to fine restaurants and on weekend getaways to the mountains. He was never anything less than a gentleman and could always make her laugh.

But whenever she brought up the *Magic* tournament that she was entering or the latest superhero crossover, he would always change the subject. Whenever he would spend the night at her apartment she could always see him giving weird eyes to the horror movie posters on her walls and the anime figurines decorating her bookshelf.

It was after they had been dating for a month that he asked her, "What do you see in all that . . . fantasy stuff?"

"First off, I'm more into sci-fi and horror than fantasy and second . . ." she paused. "It's fun."

He nodded thoughtfully. "But what else do you want?"

"What do you mean?"

"What are your hopes and dreams? Your goals?"

She poked with her fork at the expensive meal before her. "I don't know yet."

***

They had been dating for six months. Things had been going wonderfully and Janice and Vash were becoming a real couple—going everywhere together, spending every night together, and learning to tolerate each other's foibles. He kept his ranting of stock market variations to himself and she did the same with price guide listings of Sega Genesis games.

On their anniversary date he asked her, "How do you feel about kids?"

The question took her off guard. She considered it and then said, with a smile, "It depends on the person."

***

Three months later he asked her to marry him. She couldn't believe it. It was what she wanted, someone to love her always. They talked and planned that they would have to move in together. They should get a house, property was cheap in Stewartstown and there would be plenty of space for rug rats.

She called her mother and texted Benny and Gary, her gamer friends at Brave Nerd World about the good news.

After a few conversations and browsing of the newspaper classifieds, they knew they would need a rather large chunk of money. Vash could easily pay for it all, and offered to, but Janice wasn't going to be supported by anyone, not even her soon-to-be husband.

"I know how I can get my share of the money," she said.

***

It took her two months but she managed to sell every comic book, video game, action figure, trading card, print, DVD, and book that she owned. She managed to raise her half of the money for the house they had their eyes on.

She sat on the couch in her apartment and looked around at the bare shelves and walls. Before, those were the things that would fill her with happiness and satisfaction. There was a time that she would have never imagined her life without all those objects. But now, she found herself smiling at the emptiness. It actually represented how full her life was about to be.

***

Janice and Vash sat before the doctor holding hands. He didn't look happy.

"I'm sorry Ms. Chapel," he said. "The tests came back and they don't look good. You're never going to be able to have children."

It was weird hearing those words. She never felt very strongly about having kids. The idea had crossed her mind from time to time, to have little ones around that she could play Pokemon with and expose to Godzilla movies.

But Vash wanted them so badly. She felt the grip of his hand loosen so she held him tighter.

She turned to him. "I'm so sorry. You know I love you."

***

Janice sat on her couch and looked around the empty walls and shelves of her apartment. They looked exactly how she felt. She had been sitting up all night on the couch staring

83

at those blank walls. All she could think about was how she wished she still had her comics, games, books, or anything to pass the time.

Her phone buzzed and she picked it up. It was a text from Benny—he was on his way to pick her up for the convention. She responded, set the phone back down and looked around the barren room.

So this is the rest of my life . . .

12
VALLEY OF THE TRIBBLES

They were somewhere around Moab on the edge of the desert when they first saw the tribbles. Having driven through the plains and over mountains, the land became flat and dry. It was sporadic at first, small round balls of fuzz here and there along the edge of the road. But as the strong wind blew them around, the small fluffy balls increased in number.

"What are those things?" said Janice peering through the windshield.

"I'm not sure," said Benny. He eased his foot off the gas. "They look like furry tumbleweeds."

The tires of the van thumped over one of them. A loud squeal pierced their ears. Benny pulled the van over to see what had happened.

"There's blood," he said, climbing out of the van with a bewildered expression.

Gary picked up a stick and poked at the small blob of blood and fur on the road. "I think it's alive," said Gary. "I mean, it was alive. The furry things are animals."

"Tribbles," said Janice.

Benny and Gary looked over at her and she was holding one of the fur balls in her hands. It rocked gently back and forth on her palms while calmly purring.

"They're tribbles," she said again, looking up at them with glee in her eyes.

"I'm going to have to drive more careful," said Benny.

They got back in the van and Gary noticed that Janice was still carrying the tribble.

"Are you bringing that?" he asked.

She shrugged. "It's cute. Like Squishy must have looked like when she was a kitten."

Janice looked back at Squishy, who was lying on the

back floor of the van. Squishy looked at her and burped.

"You can't bring that," said Gary.

"Why not?" said Janice.

"Are you crazy? We bring one tribble in here and soon we'll have a dozen and then a hundred. There will be tribbles in every little corner. We'll never get them out."

"We really don't need a bunch of little tribbles rolling around," said Benny.

"OK," said Janice. She opened the van and gently placed the furball on the ground.

Benny pulled the van back on the road, making sure not to smoosh any more tribbles.

***

Below a round sign that said Skaro Depot, the van pulled up to a gas pump. As they slid open the van door, a strong hot breeze blew through, carrying with it the sounds of tribbles purring. At hearing the strange sound, Squishy hopped out. She waddled to one of the balls of fluff. She began batting at it with her paw and the tribble rocked back and forth, purring loudly.

Benny tapped the pump. "It's shut off."

They all looked at the small shack that served as the store. "I guess we're going in."

Janice and Gary nodded. They approached with slow and careful steps, wary that at any moment some threat would present itself.

Gary reached forward and grabbed the door knob. There was a window in the door but it was frosted glass—the only way for them to find out what was inside was to go in.

Gary, still gripping the knob, looked at Benny and Janice. Their weapons were lost in Riverside and the van didn't have anything useful for defense. They felt painfully naked but there was no other option.

"Ready?" asked Gary.

They nodded.

"OK, then on three, two, one," and he opened the door.

They cautiously stepped into the store. It was small, just four aisles and one freezer, but it was stocked with the normal snacks and road travel necessities.

"At least we got lucky this time," said Benny, moving to the store counter. "I'll get the gas going."

"Gary, give me a hand," said Janice as she began to grab food from the shelves.

"I hope there's some beer," he said heading for the freezer.

There was a door in the corner of the store behind the counter that they had not noticed. It led to the back of the building and at that moment it slammed open. Benny, Gary, and Janice all froze and whipped their heads at the sound of the noise.

A robot came rolling in. It looked like someone had turned a trashcan upside down. It had two short extensions halfway up its "body"—one looked like a toilet plunger, the other like a wire whisk. On top of the machine was something like a flashlight. They all knew their sci-fi and knew immediately what they were looking at—a Dalek.

Its head piece swiveled back and forth and they waited for it to blast them.

"SERVICE," it said in a monotone static voice. "SERVICE."

They looked at each other and Benny was the first to speak, "Uhhh . . . we'd like to get some gas."

"GAS," said the Dalek and it pushed a button on the counter with one of its extensions. "PUMP THREE IS ON."

"Uhhh, OK. Thanks." Gary turned back to Janice and Gary, "I guess this one's friendly."

"WOULD YOU LIKE A TASTE OF SWEET POTATO PIE?"

"Sweet potato pie?" asked Janice.

"I MADE IT MYSELF. PIES ARE SIX-FIFTY, SIX-FIFTY. SAMPLES ARE FREE, SAMPLES ARE FREE."

The Dalek spun around turning its back to them and then spun back. It carried a plate with several very small slices of orange pie.

"I'd love some," said Janice.

"Sure," said Gary.

"No thanks," said Benny.

"Come on," said Janice. "He seems okay."

"I just can't stand sweet potatoes. No thanks."

Janice shrugged. "Suit yourself."

"FORKS," said the Dalek and it spun around and then back, placing two forks on the plate.

"Thank you," said Janice picking up a fork and tasting the pie. "Mmmm, this is delicious."

"Wow," said Gary with a mouthful. "This is really good."

"WHOLE PIES ARE SIX FIFTY. SAMPLES ARE FREE," said the Dalek

Janice and Gary nodded as they continued to eat the pie.

Then it suddenly boomed, "EXTERMINATE."

They all jumped at the Dalek's signature war cry, each expecting the robot to blast them with its kill-ray. Instead it quickly zoomed around the counter and turned to face the entrance.

In the open doorway, two tribbles had rolled in. They were each twitching back and forth, slowly making their way deeper into the store.

"EXTERMINATE," said the Dalek. The extension that looked like a wire whisk started to glow blue and then it fired off two blasts, each hitting a tribble. The tribbles briefly glowed blue, there was a flash of white light, and they turned into small piles of gray ash.

"EXTERMINATE," it said again, this time with a hint of satisfaction and then moved back behind the counter.

"I have to admit," said Gary, still eating pie. "That makes a lot of sense."

"Daleks and tribbles. This apocalypse has a lot of continuity issues," said Janice.

Gary nodded. "Not to mention copyright headaches."

"At this point I think we're firmly in parody territory," said Benny. "I'm gonna go fill up the van, you guys load up."

Benny walked through the lot over to the van. Sure enough, the pump's LCD screen was on. He started pumping gas. The air was warm but the constant breeze kept it from being uncomfortably hot. The sound of tribbles purring was constant in the background and the soft sound made him feel relaxed.

The convention seemed like a thousand years ago, and they had been fighting for their lives since. It was nice to get a break. He smiled as he watched Squishy, still fascinated with the tribble she found, pawing at and circling the strange creature.

The pump dinged and he put the nozzle back. He walked away from the pumps while taking out his pack of cigarettes. He put a smoke in his mouth and lit up. He closed his eyes and exhaled, savoring this moment of peace.

He absent mindedly smoked and looked to the store. He had left the door open when he walked out so he could know if anything went bad in the store. Janice and Gary were still inside loading up food, drinks, and other goods.

He suddenly felt an extreme unease. He noticed that the tribbles had stopped purring. Instead of a low, happy rubble, the air was filled with a quiet hiss from the small creatures.

He looked back at Squishy. She was no longer playing with the tribble and was now sitting up. Ears back, she stared off down the highway in the direction of Riverside.

"What's up girl?" he said and walked past her.

Benny moved closer to the highway and looked off in the distance. At first he didn't notice anything. The tribbles blew across the road and their sounds filled the air. Then he saw it. In the distance, there was a dark brown cloud on the highway. The cloud got larger as he watched. His first thought was a sand storm, but then he knew what he was really looking at.

The tribbles started to hiss louder.

"Fuck," he mumbled and threw down his cigarette. He ran as fast as he could to Squishy, who was still looking off intently into the distance, and snatched her into his arms. He ran into the store.

Gary and Janice looked up, surprised and concerned to see Benny holding Squishy and panting.

"What's wrong," asked Janice.

"We got company," said Benny.

Then they heard the sounds of engines. At first it was low and just barely noticeable and then it got louder and louder and louder. It was distinctly the sound of motorcycles and it sounded like there were hundreds coming their way.

Soon the motorcycles were upon them. Dozens came roaring into the parking lot and pulling up to the pumps, and there were still obviously many more on their way.

Benny peeked out the doorway and muttered.

"Shit, shit, shit."

All the bikers had prosthetic ridges on their foreheads. He slammed the door shut and backed further into the store clutching Squishy tighter.

"What is it?" asked Janice, worry in her voice.

"It's Koloth and he's made a lot of new friends."

After a few minutes the sounds of motorcycles pulling up finally ceased. There had to be hundreds of them out there. They could hear the sounds of people talking and laughing and bikes being parked.

With all the noise, they didn't hear the people walking up until they were just outside. The door burst open and two bikers marched in. They were each burly and covered in white power tattoos. The sun and heat had been hard on their forehead ridges and the rubber was pulling back at the edges.

They each were holding hand guns, out and ready to fire.

"Well looka what we has here," said one of the bikers through a mouth missing at least half of its teeth.

"SERVICE," said the Dalek.

The bikers said nothing and moved closer to Benny, Gary, and Janice while they backed into the corner of the store.

"Yo, look at what they're wearing," said the other biker. All three of them, and Squishy, were still wearing their Star Fleet uniforms, now torn in many places and stained with blood and dirt.

"You think they're who the boss was looking for?"

"Yeah. I do."

Both bikers leered at Janice.

"Yeah, that's them. That's the girl the boss wants. I see why."

Both bikers laughed.

"SERVICE."

"Fuck off tin can."

The bikers moved forward. "Now you can walk out with us, or we can make this fun."

The Dalek moved from behind the counter to the center of the store. "THERE WILL BE NO DISTURBANCES IN THIS STORE."

The bikers froze and turned, their faces displaying obvious disbelief.

"Oh yeah, and what the fuck are you going to do about it?" said the biker with the missing tooth.

"EXTERMINATE," it said, and its death-ray glowed blue and fired off a shot. In an instant the biker, his clothes and his weapon were nothing more than a pile of ash.

"Fuck," said the other biker. He ran out of the store, the door swinging shut behind him.

Benny, Gary, and Janice moved from out of the corner and they couldn't help but stare at the pile of ash.

"Dude," said Gary. "Thanks man."

Benny was looking in the direction of the door and what sounded like hundreds of people talking, yelling, and revving bikes.

"But what about all of them out there?" he said.

"THERE WILL BE NO DISTURBANCES."

"I'm not sure they think the same," said Janice.

A few long minutes passed and then they heard more footsteps from outside. The door swung open again and this time three Klingon bikers walked in—the same one that had just run out, a skinny guy with meth-sores all over his face and long ratty hair, and Koloth himself. Squishy hissed at them from Benny's arms.

"Well, well, well," Koloth said oozing confidence. "Look at who we have here."

He smiled a pointy toothed grin. He must have filed his teeth to points since the last time they saw him at the rest stop. His smiled got bigger when his eyes landed on Janice. She thought he looked like a shark.

"SERVICE."

Koloth turned to the Dalek, "Yes, we would very much like some service. We've been traveling long and our bikes and bellies are empty."

"WOULD YOU LIKE A TASTE OF SWEET POTATO PIE?"

"Maybe later," Koloth said. He turned back to Benny, Gary, and Janice, "Why don't you three step outside with me? I'd like to . . . talk."

"Your friends don't look like the talking type," said Benny.

"Don't be judgmental," sneered Koloth. "Come on outside."

"No," said Benny.

"You really want to make this difficult?" said Koloth. "Bring them," he said to the other two bikers.

They started to move forward.

"YOU MAY HAVE SERVICE. YOU MAY NOT HARASS OTHER CUSTOMERS," said the Dalek.

"We're not harassing," said Koloth. "We just want to have a chat with our friends."

"You're no friend of ours," said Janice

"YOU MAY HAVE SERVICE. YOU MAY NOT HARASS OTHER CUSTOMERS," said the Dalek.

Koloth nodded, "I understand." He turned to the other two bikers, "I guess we do this the hard way."

Koloth moved with sudden speed, dropping down and moving behind the other bikers while they stepped forward. The two bikers each raised a handgun. Behind the Dalek, the door to the back of the building burst open and a third biker with a shotgun stepped inside. All three opened fire, the sound of three guns going off in the small store was deafening.

The bullets and pellets bounced off the Dalek and ricocheted through the store.

"EXTERMINATE." The Dalek spun around and fired off

three shots from its death-ray and turned all three attackers to dust while Koloth ran out the door.

The Dalek came from behind the counter yet again and headed to the door. It paused and turned its headpiece to face Benny, Gary, and Janice.

"FOLLOW."

And then it was out the door.

They moved slowly out from behind the shelves and apprehensively followed the Dalek. The Dalek left the door open so they could see outside. There were at least a hundred bikers outside all visibly armed.

The Dalek was only a few feet outside the building when dozens of guns went off. Bikers fired on it from every direction. Spectacularly, all the shots bounced off it and there was no sign of damage.

The Dalek spun around with surprising speed and fired off shots of its own in every direction. Bikers everywhere were quickly reduced to ash. But not all the shots were directed at people. Some of the blasts hit bikes and they exploded in balls of fire and shrapnel. A few of the blasts hit some tribbles rolling around the lot, because the Dalek fucking hated tribbles.

The bikers kept shooting and so did the Dalek. Eventually, Koloth's voice could be heard shouting out, "Cease fire! Cease fire!"

Once the bikers stopped, so did the Dalek.

"YIPPEE KI-YAY MOTHERFUCKER," said the Dalek. It turned its head around to the store. "FOLLOW."

It began zooming calmly forward. Benny, Gary, and Janice followed it out into the parking lot.

They could instantly feel all the hateful eyes on them. The parking lot, and the highway, and the surrounding fields were full of bikers and their rides, like it was some kind of convention. Most had guns, knives, or a weapon of some sort. And they were all staring at them.

The Dalek came to a stop and its headpiece slowly swiveled around. "THERE WILL BE NO DISTURBANCES," it announced.

Koloth stepped out from behind their van—he had been using it for cover in the shoot-out. He had his hands raised to show he was unarmed.

"OK, OK," he said while walking over to them. "There will be no disturbances. But we do desperately need gas."

"YOU MAY HAVE SERVICE."

"And we want them," Koloth pointed at Gary, Janice and Benny.

"YOU MAY NOT DISTURB OTHER CUSTOMERS."

Koloth frowned. "So how's this going to work then?"

"YOU WILL LET THE CUSTOMERS LEAVE WITHOUT INCIDENT AND THEN I WILL ATTEND TO YOUR SERVICE."

Koloth considered the statement and shrugged.

"Alright."

He then started yelling loudly enough for the bikers around to hear but never took his eyes off them.

"Our friends here are going to leave and no one is going to bother them. Everyone understand? Remember, your honor is at stake."

The Dalek spun its headpiece around to address Benny, Gary, and Janice.

"GATHER YOUR PURCHASES. THEY ARE FREE OF CHARGE. I APOLOGIZE FOR ANY INCONVENIENCES."

They ran back into the store and grabbed as much as they could carry—jerky, dried fruit, smokes, beer, water, and anything else that seemed useful. Then they walked back out, past the Dalek and several small piles of ash.

"Thanks," said Benny.

"HAVE A NICE DAY," replied the Dalek.

They all locked eyes as they walked past Koloth to get to the van. A hissing tribble was blown by the wind and came to a stop right in front of Koloth. He slammed his heavy boot down and the furry critter exploded like a water balloon filled with strawberry jam.

"You're not getting away," Koloth said quietly, so the Dalek wouldn't hear.

"Sure looks like it to me," responded Gary.

"I have an army."

"We have a Dalek."

Koloth smiled. "Not once you leave here."

His breath smelled like dog food.

They ignored him and climbed into the van.

"No one bother them," Koloth yelled out to the other bikers.

Benny started the van and began to slowly pull out of the lot, bikers moving aside to make room. Gary and Squishy looked out the back window. Gary raised his middle finger and lifted one of Squishy's paws with his other arm. They both "flipped off" Koloth.

The van got on the road and headed west. Koloth watched them drive away until their van was little more than a dot on the horizon. He turned to the Dalek.

"Alright, now about those services you keep babbling about."

"SERVICE," said the Dalek as it turned and zoomed back to the store.

13
THE CITY ON THE EDGE OF THE PAST

They were nervous for the next few hours of driving, they kept a constant watch out of the back window of the van but there was never a sign that they were being followed. The bikers must have been telling the truth and really needed gas.

"Holy shit," said Gary from the back.

"What?" yelled Benny and Janice in unison, immediately expecting news of an attack.

"I found a tape!"

One of the worst parts of the drive in the van was that there was nothing to listen to. Even if they hadn't left all the CDs in the broken down DeLorean, the van only had a tape deck. Of course there was no radio, so all they had to pass the time was conversation. One quickly finds that when it's the end of the world and you're driving through desert that there isn't much to talk about.

"Pass it up," said Janice.

Gary did and Benny popped it into the tape deck. Immediately the van was filled with the loud dissonant noise of lightning fast guitars and drums. A Japanese man with a nasally slurring voice screamed over it.

Benny popped out the tape.

"What the hell was that?" asked Janice.

"Mouthful of Ants," he said, reading the label on the cassette.

"Sounds like it," said Gary from the back.

They drove on in silence for a few more miles. Janice was the first to speak again when she spotted something ahead.

"I think I see someone."

Benny squinted his eyes and, sure enough, there was a figure ahead standing on the side of the road waving his arms. He slowed down the van and scanned the countryside. It was nothing but flat desert with mountains in the distance. There appeared to be no one around but the lone figure.

Two suitcases lay on the ground by the man's side. He was dressed in a brown suit with a brown top hat. As they got closer they could see that his clothes were torn in many places. His face was covered with cuts and scrapes and his right eye was swollen shut by a large blue bruise.

"So what do you think?" asked Benny.

"No way," said Gary from the back. "Guy's probably psycho."

Benny looked to Janice.

"I think he's hurt," said Janice.

"So what," said Gary. "Not our problem."

"We should help him," said Janice. "He's out here in the middle of nowhere."

"Exactly, how'd he get out here?"

"Let's find out," said Benny pulling the van over.

"Seriously, dude?" said Gary. "Well don't come crying to me when he makes a mask out of your face."

Gary slid the side door open.

"I cannot express how grateful I am for you to have stopped for this lonely and battered soul." He spoke with an obviously fake British accent. He smiled at them, two of his front teeth were missing.

"No so quick," said Gary. "You some kinda nutcase? Are you going to kill us all and steal the van? Because we're not having that."

"No, good sir," said the man. "I am not a threat to you. Though I cannot speak the same of those scoundrels on their motorized bicycles."

"Koloth?" said Janice to Benny. She turned to the man. "Was it a large group on motorcycles that did this to you?" She motioned to his eye.

"Indeed, the brutes."

"Okay," said Gary. "But no funny stuff."

"I wouldn't think of it," said the man.

He picked up his two suitcases and climbed in the van.

He winced and held his side as he sat down.

They got a better look at what he was wearing, it was a normal brown man's suit but it was decorated with metal gears where there should've been buttons. While the man wore small-framed glasses, which matched his goatee nicely, there were a large set of goggles around his top hat.

"What a blistering day," he said smiling and held out his hand. "My name is Neville Ruffington."

They introduced themselves.

"So where are you headed?" asked Benny.

"Back to the promised land," said Neville, smiling. "Fort Galdsden."

"OK . . . where's that?"

"Just a few hours down the road."

"What's Fort Galdsden?" asked Janice.

"Oh, it's a wonderful place. A refuge for like-minded souls from all the chaos that we currently find ourselves in. With plenty of food, drink, and shelter."

"Uh-huh."

"What's in the suitcases?" asked Gary.

Neville picked one up and set it on his lap. He popped the case open and turned it to display to everyone in the van. It was almost overflowing with candy. Skittles, Milky Way, Butterfinger, Nerds, and many other varieties. Squishy sniffed at the case.

Neville explained, "While we manage to sustain ourselves quite nicely, there are still the treats we miss. There is a nice metal man who runs a shop, in the direction you originated from in fact, that supplies us with these confectionary vices."

"We met him," said Gary. "He was a cool dude."

"Indeed."

"So, how'd you get there?" asked Janice.

"I've been walking. It was quite the arduous trip by foot which is why I am, once again, so grateful for your assistance. Once we arrive, you must stay. For at least a bit. We have much we can offer and it is the least I can do for your generosity."

Benny, Janice, and Gary exchanged knowing glances.

"There's one more thing I gotta ask," said Gary. "Your people, they don't . . . kill other people? Or hold sacrifices or anything like that?"

"Oh, goodness no."

"Then it's gotta be better than the last place we crashed at."

"So you had a run in with the bikers?" asked Benny.

"You could call it that," said Neville. "Their caravan passed me by yesterday. I minded my own business and assumed they would let me attend to mine. But six came back and gave me a mighty thrashing. They abandoned me out in the desert—took the night to recover enough to trek back to the road."

"They left you in the desert?" said Janice.

"I lost consciousness when I took a nasty pipe to the head." He took off his hat and his temple was covered with dried blood. "I imagine they thought me dead."

"Dude, does that hurt?" said Gary.

"Quite," said Neville as he put the hat back on.

"So you say you live with other people?" asked Janice.

"Oh my yes," said Neville. He pulled a Milky War out of his pocket and unwrapped it. "We are numbering at least five hundred at this point."

"Five hundred people out here? In the middle of the desert?" said Benny.

"We are attempting to build a new world on the ruins of the old."

"What kind of new world do you have in mind?"

"We are dedicated to a philosophy of pursuing the intellectual and technological arts. But we are modeled after a time before gasoline, electricity, and modern culture subverted and perverted the noblest endeavors. That is what killed our world, our loss of innocence."

"What does that all mean?" asked Benny.

"We're all steampunks, good fellow," said Neville as he took a large bite from the candy bar.

"Steampunk?" said Gary. "Isn't that when Goths discovered the color brown and Etsy?

"I don't know," said Janice. "I think Steampunk is kinda

cool. I like the handmade stuff. Did you make that?"

She pointed at a bracelet that was poking out from beneath Neville's coat sleeve.

"Of course," he said and rolled up his sleeve so they could get a better look.

The bracelet was made of thick black leather about five inches wide and decorated with gold gears and brass latches. The front had three clock faces with the gears exposed. There were no numbers for the time and just one long hand instead of the normal two.

"What does it do?" asked Gary.

"It measures local electro-magnetic pulse frequencies. The top meter tells me local atmospheric saturation. The middle monitors variation frequency. And the bottom is risk variance. As you can see, all are reading normal."

"What the hell? What's the point of that?" said Gary. "So, how does it work?"

"Well . . . it really doesn't."

***

After driving for two hours on the highway, Neville directed Benny to make a left turn. Benny didn't even see the road at first, it was little more than a dirt path. They went along the bumpy path for an hour and then they saw Fort Galdsden.

A massive wooden wall, at least thirty feet high and five hundred feet wide, wrapped around whatever it was protecting. There were figures at the top of the wall every couple dozen feet keeping watch. In the center of the wall was a giant gate.

"Pull up and let me out to talk to them," directed Neville.

Benny did. He got out and one of the figures shouted down (also with a fake British accent), "Halt! Who goes there?"

"It is I, Neville, with our sweets!

"Neville?" shouted back the voice. "We feared the worst when you did not return yesterday."

"Not yet. I have three good souls that aided me. They

have been traveling long and deserve a moment of respite."

Neville got back in the van and the gate opened. Benny drove them in and the gate shut behind them.

Once inside, it was obvious that Neville was telling the truth and this was indeed a community. Wooden buildings, all with chimneys billowing smoke or steam, lined the main road. Men, women, and children hurried about the inside of the complex, caught up in their own duties. The men all wore brown suits and most had matching tophats. The women wore black frilly dresses and corsets. Many of the villagers paused to stare in amazement as their van slowly drove past.

Neville directed them to pull over next to one of the buildings. They all got out of the van, Squishy in Benny's satchel, and once the people saw the Star Trek uniforms, they stared even more.

"Come," said Neville heading to the front door of the main building. "Come meet the Lord Mayor."

With some trepidation, they followed him in.

They walked into a large open room with lots of long tables, not too different from a cafeteria.

"This is the town hall," Neville explained. "The Lord Mayor's office is in the back."

They followed him around the tables to a small hallway in the back corner of the room. It led to several doors that looked like they lead to offices. The back hallway ended at one door which Neville knocked on. A voice called, "Enter!"

They walked into the room. A portly bald man wearing a brown suit sat behind a desk. A large bushy mustache obscured his lips and there was a monocle over his right eye. His left eye was covered by a bronze cone that came to a point about four inches from his face. The end was clear glass, with a hint of eye visible through the cone. The contraption was held in place by straps that wrapped around his head.

"Neville? How good to see you have returned, I had fears. But what happened to you that you sustained such injuries?" He was another that spoke with a fake British accent.

"Some bandits up to no good trounced me mightily. But

fear not, the injuries are but surface. Though I fear I may need a day or two of rest."

"Of course," said the Lord Mayor. "You have undoubtedly earned it." He turned to Benny, Gary, and Janice. "And who are these new faces?"

"These good Samaritans gave me transport. I fear that without their assistance, in my weakened state, the elements would have surely done me in."

"Then we are in your debt," said the Lord Mayor.

He wheeled out from behind his desk. He was in a motorized wheelchair. All of its plastic and metal parts had been covered up with ply board and clock parts.

"I am Lord Mayor Brunkshire." He shook their hands and they introduced themselves.

"How can we repay you for your kindness" said Brunkshire. "Please, stay and rest for a spell."

"We're headed somewhere but I think we can stay for a bit," said Benny.

"I would love to sleep in a real bed again," said Janice.

"That we have," said Brunkshire.

"You better not try to eat us," said Gary.

"Eat you?" said Brunkshire. "That would not be the English thing to do." He turned to Benny, "But I must admit to curiosity. You mentioned a trip. What brings you out here to these desolate lands?"

"Ummm, well," Benny paused. "We're on our way to Los Angeles. We're going to save William Shatner."

Brunkshire nodded. "A noble venture. But personally, I always preferred Patrick Stewart."

***

They ate dinner in the large room they had walked through to find the Lord Mayor's office. Every seat at each table was filled with people and they all spoke with fake British accents. Dinner was beef stew with biscuits. Benny, Gary, and Janice all had seats at the head of the middle table, right next to Lord Mayor Brunkshire. Even Squishy had a place, her face submerged in the stew. She occasionally brought up her face and brown beef broth dripped onto the table. She wheezed and snorted and then went back to guzzling the stew.

"I think the cat's gonna make me sick," said Gary.

"Then stop watching her," said Benny.

"It's the sounds."

Benny turned back to the Lord Mayor. "So where do you all come from? This is kinda the middle of nowhere."

"When . . . whatever that was that happened, every citizen here had a vision of a clockwork man and woman calling to them to build a new world," said Brunkshire. "We were all drawn here in the desert; we were all pulled to this spot to create the first settlement of the new clockwork age. Before long there were many of us. Everyone works and everyone contributes."

"But how do you keep it all going?" asked Janice. "Where do you get food and water?"

"Despite the apparent harshness of the surrounding country, there is in fact a lake not more than two kilometers away. There we have irrigated fields and cattle. What we cannot provide for ourselves, the metal man can provide."

"That is all very impressive," said Benny.

"Indeed it is," nodded Brunkshire. "And you are welcome to stay as long as you wish. We are all quite grateful to your assistance of Neville."

"No offense," said Gary. "But we're ready to get to L.A."

"Yeah," agreed Janice. "Do you have any idea how long it will take us to get to L.A. from here?"

"Oh, not all that long. Just over four hours. You'll be there by midday."

"Fuckin' A," said Gary. "This is probably a stupid question, but you wouldn't happen to have any TVs lying around, would you."

"Sadly, no. We have no need for the cathode ray box and you'll find none within our walls. But it is rare that we get guests in these parts. Please, tell me of your travels and adventures across this strange new land."

They told him of the disaster at the convention and of their decision to save William Shatner. Of the cannibals in Iowa and the Zombie Borg that massacred them. And they finished with the standoff with the Klingon biker gang.

"It's distressing to hear of those ruffians so close to our borders but there is little concern of them disturbing us here. We are well fortified and protected, not to underestimate our remote location. We believe this spot was specifically chosen buy our clockwork saviors and one day, they too will come join us.

"But what marvelous tales you have. Is there anything we could offer you for your last leg of your journey?"

"If we're only a few hours away, I think we'll be good," said Benny. "The only thing I am concerned about is our gas. The van is a guzzler and we're getting pretty low."

Brunkshire smiled. "Well, why didn't you say so earlier?"

***

Brunkshire took them to one of the many hand-built wooden buildings. The doors to this building were larger than the doors to most of the other buildings and there were no windows. The doors were latched with a board, like a barn door. Two of the other community members lifted the heavy wooden board and pushed open the door.

"We've been hoarding it since the fall of society. It was so dangerous and destructive to the world. I have a suspicion that it's why the Clockwork Gods brought this down on us. We don't want others to find it and attempt to rebuild the world with poison again."

Brunkshire lead them into the building.

"It's obviously toxic—we cannot dump it into the soil, so we keep it stored here. But you are welcome to take as much as you believe your quest may need."

Benny, Gary, and Janice looked around the room. It was just one large space, bigger than a basketball court and was stacked floor to ceiling with drums of gasoline.

"Oh," said Benny. "I don't think we'll need that much."

***

On one of the nearby mountains, a Klingon biker had set up basic camp for the night. He looked through binoculars at those weird Star Trek fans that the boss was so obsessed with. They were walking into some building with one of those funny dressed people. All the people in the compound seemed like they dressed funny.

No one had spotted him on the mountain. He had no need for a fire and as long as he faced away from the compound when he hit his meth, no one would see him.

He picked up his walkie talkie and turned it on.

"I got them, they're at some kind of fort . . . I don't know, maybe five, six hundred total. Haven't seen many weapons . . . no, it should be pretty easy. I think they're all fags."

***

Koloth sat behind the counter at the gas station. They had dismantled the Dalek. He used the bottom half as a chair and his feet were propped up on the upper half.

"On our way," he said into the walkie talkie. "*Qapla'*"

He walked out of the store into the parking lot. It was buzzing with activity. The bikers had been running around gathering up as many of the tribbles as they could find. They were placing them into a huge pile in a field next to the gas station. The mound of hissing furry balls was almost ten feet high.

"Men," shouted Koloth.

The bikers all stopped their activities and turned to their leader.

"We ride at dawn," Koloth bellowed. "But first we drink!" He hoisted a bottle of beer raided from the store high in the air and his men roared.

"And we burn the tribbles!"

The men roared again as someone tossed a match onto the tribble mound. The mountain of living fur balls quivered and squealed as the flames spread.

Koloth laughed and chugged his beer while the tribbles began to scream.

14
SQUISHY'S STORY

Squishy wasn't always named Squishy and she wasn't always so fat. Once she was a little kitten, third in a litter of six. She was adopted by a loving middle-class couple for their ten-year-old son they loved so much.

She was a tiny kitten with long white fur and orange patches that poofed out in every direction. They gave her to their son on Christmas morning.

"Look at your new little friend," said the mother.

"What are you going to name her, Son?" asked the father.

The fat little boy snorted, "I don't know." He looked closely into the kitten's eyes and she wiggled and squeaked. "I'll call her Noob."

He set down the kitten and looked away. "What else did I get?"

The name would have been cute but part of the reason for it was the boy was obsessed with video games. He would start to play Call of Duty once he got home from school until his parents would make him go to bed. The little kitten would hop around his feet wishing for a dangling piece of string or hoping to be petted.

The boy would glare down at her and push her away with his feet. "Go eat," he'd say. "I'm busy."

The boy's parents made him feed Noob and give her water, to teach him responsibility. But he would only refill the dishes when her crying became too much for his parents to endure.

One day when he was racking up some major frags, Noob was playing with the cord from the Xbox. She crouched down and pounced, unplugging the controller and getting the boy's character killed.

"What the fuck," shouted the boy, standing up. "That's totally not fair."

The screen flashed the "controller disconnected" message and the boy stormed to the game console.

He looked behind the TV and saw Noob as she rolled around, biting and pawing at the controller cord. He picked her up and she purred.

"Bad cat," he shouted.

He placed her on his floor and considered what he should do. He could kick her but she was a stupid cat and might not get the message. Then he got a great idea.

He grabbed his school backpack and dumped out his books. He roughly picked her up and shoved her in. He left the house and walked to the corner and waited. Soon a bus pulled up and he got on sitting in an empty row of two seats. He placed the backpack on the seat next to him. Noob squirmed and mewed and he shook the bag to hush her.

The ride was only fifteen minutes, not too far, but far enough. He got off in the business district of town. He walked down a nearby alley and ducked behind a dumpster. Once a quick look around confirmed no one was watching, he unzipped the backpack, and dumped Noob to the ground.

She tumbled out and quickly crouched down, her little body shaking. Her green eyes were wide and she looked for reassurance.

The boy turned and walked away and never looked back. He took the bus home and went back to his game. When his parents got home from work he told them that when he got home from school the front door was open and Noob had run away.

The first two days, she was too scared to move from behind the dumpster. It was cold and it rained. Her fur was soaked, matted with mud, and fleas nipped at her. She cried for food and warmth but none came.

On the third day the hunger hurt so bad that she forgot about her fear. She was small so she could climb into dumpsters or trash cans. It took her a day of wandering and dodging traffic before she found part of a hamburger that someone was too lazy to throw away properly.

She walked the streets until the sun started to go down.

It was a small town with much of the surrounding area undeveloped, so thick woods were only a few blocks away. She found an uprooted tree that had fallen over in some past storm. There was a hollow hole in the tree that she climbed into and slept.

And that's how she lived for the next four years. Venturing into town for what scraps she could find and searching for cover at night.

She didn't know what a comic book/gaming store was, but she was happy when Brave Nerd World opened. The trash cans in back where always overflowing with bags of chips, candy, and half empty soda cans.

She loved the sweets and there always seemed to be plenty. So she would raid the trash almost daily and quickly she became bigger and rounder.

The only thing she really had to watch out for was the fat man that would come around. He had strange brown ridges on his forehead that she never saw on other humans and he always stunk of Cheetos. If he saw her he would throw rocks at her and laugh as she ran to hide.

One time she wasn't paying attention, she was engrossed in licking the dust from an empty bag of Ranch Doritos. The fat man snuck up behind her and kicked her right in the ass. The force carried her two feet through the air and she crashed, squealing into a pile of empty soda cans.

"Hehe," snorted the fat man, the fake ridges on his forehead bouncing. "Stupid fucking cat."

She ran and hid behind the dumpster where he couldn't reach. She pissed blood for a week.

She hated the fat man with ridges.

But there was another man who also came by. He would smoke cigarettes in the alley behind the store where the trash was stored.

The first time he saw her she was hiding behind the recycling bin, eyeing him and trying to figure out if it was worth the risk raiding the soda can or if she should wait.

"Hey there," he said, his voice soft.

He backed up and crouched down.

"Oh, it's okay," he held out his hand, palm up. "Come on out."

She poked her head out and cocked it at the man.

"Come on, it's okay."

She slowly crept out, her belly now so huge from the junk food that she waddled more than she walked.

"Oh my god, you're such a pretty girl."

She wobbled up to him and the man scratched her chin. She purred loudly.

That's where their relationship began. He would come outside and pet her and say nice things on his smoke break and she would purr.

Soon he began to bring her cat treats and sometimes he would even leave a dish of water. She liked him and began to live in the dumpster behind the store. She would eat all night and wait for him to show up all day.

One day, he came. He knelt down next to her, patted her head, and picked her up. She purred. He was wearing a brown satchel with a large Starfleet insignia on the flap and he gently placed her inside. He walked to the bus stop, boarded it, and took her home.

She was so happy to be inside again. He had food and water waiting for her. She immediately wobbled over to the dishes. After she ate and drank her fill, he gave her a bath, washing the stink and fleas from her fur. She didn't like that but at least she didn't itch so much anymore.

That first night, the man was sitting at his computer looking annoyed. He would type a few lines and then sigh. There was a bottle next to him and he was drinking a lot from it.

She sat watching him for a while from across the room. He had spent a lot of time fussing over her when he first brought her in but for the past few hours he had been sitting, staring at the computer screen. She could feel his aggravation from across the room.

She wobbled over to him and sat next to his chair, looking up. He paid her no attention. She got bored and wobbled around to the back of his computer. There were cords all around and she loved cords. She reached out and began batting at them. Her paw caught what happened to be the computer's power cord. She yanked, but it was wrapped around her and she couldn't get free. So she pulled harder and it popped out of the computer, shutting it down.

"What the fuck?" yelled the man as he leapt to his feet.

He looked around the back of his computer. She was crouched down, shaking, looking up with big eyes waiting for his anger.

He saw her with the power cord still wrapped around her paw and he smiled. He picked her up and cuddled her close.

He carried her across the room and sat down on the bed with her in his lap.

"What am I going to do with you?" he said. He held her up and looked into her eyes. "What is your name anyway? God, you're a fat furry thing."

He hugged her and she burped.

"You've got such a big squishy belly, it's ridiculous." He laughed. "Squishy. It's got a nice ring to it. What do you think?"

She purred.

Squishy was happy.

15
STEAMPUNK
PARADISE LOST

The next morning they woke and had breakfast. It was plain oatmeal, but better than the candy or beef jerky they were used to scavenging. They used the siphons and filled up their van and loaded two additional cans of gas to be safe.

"I can't thank you enough for your generosity," said Benny.

"Please," said Brunkshire. "It is our pleasure."

"Well, all the same, it's still really nice to meet some people who aren't trying to kill us," said Gary.

"Good luck on your ventures and send my regards to Mr. Shatner."

Then bells began to ring.

Brunkshire's chair turned to face the front gates, concern riddled his face.

"What's that?" asked Benny.

"Something's wrong."

Benny ran to the van where Squishy was. He grabbed his satchel with the cat inside. Then they headed in the direction of the alarm.

As they approached the gates, they began to hear another sound —the low rumble of many motorcycles. Benny, Gary, and Janice exchanged looks.

"Fuck," mumbled Benny.

They reached the gates and there was no mistaking the sound. The army of Klingon Bikers was on the other side.

"What seems to be the problem?" called Brunkshire up to the lookouts.

"Ummm . . . Lord Mayor," shouted down one of the lookouts, his British accent slipping with his nerves. "I believe you should come up here and see this."

Brunkshire moved to the scaffolding that led to the

lookout points and Benny, Gary, and Janice followed.

He stopped and turned to them. "You should stay down here, until the situation has resolved itself."

"If it's who we think it is, you might want us up there," said Gary.

Brunkshire cocked his head and then nodded.

He drove his chair to a wooden platform on the ground and turned around to face them. "Well, get on."

They got on the platform and, with a hard jerk that rocked them all, it rose up the wall. The lift belched out steam from beneath that drifted up and around them.

The mountains rose on both sides of the valley and looked like sleeping giants buried in the sand. It would have been picturesque and beautiful if it weren't for what was waiting outside the gates for them.

About two hundred motorcycles were revving their engines. The gang,—no Koloth was right—the *army* was armed with guns, chains, and pipes. Each member had Klingon forehead ridges that were visible from even this distance.

"Are these the men that you told of last night?" asked Brunkshire.

They nodded.

Brunkshire turned to the lookouts and gave a signal with his hand. They lifted trumpets that had been hanging from their side and blew. The lookouts that had not seen the signal heard the trumpets, and then blew their own, joining in.

Then they all stopped. In the compound, the people that were milling about in the streets, waiting to find out what was going on. At the trumpet signal, they all ran off the streets into the surrounding buildings.

"What's going on?" asked Janice.

Brunkshire smiled. "We can defend ourselves."

The bikes suddenly all cut their engines at once and everyone turned their attention to the sieging army.

A voice boomed over an air horn, Benny, Gary, and Janice all recognized it immediately as Koloth. It took them a moment to locate him in the mass, but there he was, in the dead center.

"Leaders of this compound, we come before you here

honorably. This looks to be a fine home you are building for yourself. We do not wish to harm you or your home. We just want the Trekkies. Give them to us and we will walk way. Do not make us unleash our dogs of war. You will regret it."

Benny looked at Brunkshire, half expecting him to immediately hand them over. Instead he met Benny's eyes.

"Do not worry, my friend," he said.

"Well what the fuck are we going to do?" said Gary. "Koloth is starting to get obsessive."

"Like I said earlier," replied Brunkshire, "we can defend ourselves." He turned away from the gang and looked into the compound. They turned and saw what he meant.

The steampunkers who had all ran inside were now back out, all heading in the direction of the front gate. Each was holding a thin sword, the type a nobleman would be proud to bear. In addition to arming themselves, they had also changed. The men now wore steel monocles and brass top hats. The women had brass corsets elaborately decorated with clock parts.

"Swords?" exclaimed Janice. She pointed at the elaborate clockwork gun hanging from a holster at Brunkshire's side. "Why aren't you loading up your guns?"

"Ma'am, these are but decorations. There isn't a real gun in the fort."

"We're fucking dead," said Gary underneath his breath.

Brunkshire turned back to the gang. "We will not back down to you brutes."

***

Koloth smiled at the foolish man's defiance. He turned to his army. "Kill the men. Have your way with the women. Bring me the Star Fleet bitch. And extra rations for anyone that gets the head of that fucking cat"

His soldiers roared and gunned their bikes. They sped forward to meet their combatants.

"Today is a good day to die," Koloth bellowed.

16
KOLOTH OF THE
HOUSE OF GORM'S STORY

When the disaster hit the convention and everyone fled the *Magic* tournament, Koloth stayed in place. He wasn't going to run. There was still a game to finish. Koloth stayed seated before the cards.

"Guys, come on," he whined. But soon the room was empty and he was by himself.

"Fucking quitters," he mumbled under his breath and scooped up his deck. He placed the cards into his deck box and packed them safely away in his fanny pack.

He calmly stood up and walked through the tournament room. He occasionally stopped to check out the cards left behind on tables, but there was nothing worth stealing. He had better shit at home. He was playing with a bunch of amateurs that day.

He walked into the hotel's lobby and it was filled with people trying to escape. Black smoke hung thick in the air and the fires spread. There were so many people trying to get out, the front doors were just a mass of bodies. Nobody was moving out, the human mass was completely jammed. Those at the very front were already crushed and dead.

Koloth scoffed at the idiots and calmly walked down one of the side hallways and out a side exit. It never occurred to him to let anyone else know of the other exit.

The parking lot was another scene of panic and death. But Koloth just walked through it and out onto the street. He walked down the road while balls of fire crashed down from the sky and the convention center burned.

After a few blocks he came to a convenience store. He had been walking for at least fifteen minutes and needed some soda, cheese curls, and a pack of Skittles.

He was walking through the parking lot when the rumble

of motorcycles made him pause.

Tearing down the street were five bikers. They were going fast and within moments they pulled into the parking lot.

The five men were dressed head to toe in black leather and denim.

A skinny man with long black hair saw Koloth and he sneered. He rode his bike over and circled around Koloth.

"What are you supposed to be? Some kinda faggot?"

Koloth ignored the biker and stared straight ahead determined to keep his dignity.

"What's up fatty? Pig got your tongue?" The biker laughed and kept going in circles around Koloth.

His friends had now noticed he was missing and they too drove over.

"What's the hold-up, Freebase?" asked another biker with a shaved head and open drug sores across his face.

"Check out this faggot," said the first biker. He must have been "Freebase."

"Whoa," said another biker with a face filled with studded piercings. His lips, nose, cheeks, and eyebrows were covered with glittering metal. "What's on his face?"

Koloth knew he was asking about the ridges on his forehead but he still did not talk back to them. He was petrified. If their black leather and piercings weren't intimidating enough, the fact that they were covered in white power tattoos, red swastikas, grey iron crosses, and black pentagrams made him really nervous.

"Why the fuck is he dressed like that?" shouted a biker from behind that Koloth couldn't see. He was referring to the elaborate Klingon costume that Koloth had hand-tailored for himself. It had taken him years to get the costume good enough that he felt comfortable wearing it out in public but it would always be a work in progress as he tinkered and improved the design.

"He's a Klingon," said a biker with a green mohawk and dark shades.

"What's a Kling-on?" said the pierced-up biker.

"You know, from *Star Trek*," explained the mohawked biker. "The Enterprise was always having to save the day from them."

"*Star Trek?* How do you know about that nerd shit?" shouted Freebase.

"I would always watch it with my dad after he let Uncle Jim pork him when the poker games were over."

"That's fucked-up."

"Nah, it's a pretty good show."

"Enough," said the fifth biker and the only one yet to speak. He pulled the bike up in front of Koloth, shut it down, and got off. The man had the build and height of a professional wrestler, his skin adorned in ink depicting crude black stick figures dying and bathroom wall quality women showing their tits. He walked forward and stopped just inches from Koloth.

Koloth couldn't help but step back. He was tall, but this biker was huge, approaching seven feet. He glared down at Koloth, his face a mess of metal with numerous piercings through his lips, nose, ears, and eyebrows.

The other bikers pulled up behind the man and turned off their vehicles.

"Whatcha wanna do with him boss?" asked the one with the mohawk.

"Shut up," the tall biker said without looking back. "That's a nice blade you got there."

At first, Koloth thought the biker was making fun of his cardboard bat'leth that was strapped to his back but his voice was free of irony. Koloth instinctively reached around to feel his bat'leth and where he expected to feel cardboard, he instead felt hard steel. He pulled out the weapon and was amazed to find that it had turned real. In his hands was a gleaming, razor-sharp bat'leth.

"Yeah, that's real nice," said the biker pulling out a handgun and pointing it at Koloth's head. "You don't see blades like that too often. Give it to me."

Behind the bikers, the convenience store exploded and a sound like a beached whale pierced the air. The bikers all turned their heads to see what was happening, even the leader who had the gun pointed at Koloth.

Koloth took advantage of the moment and sliced through the tall biker's stomach with the bat'leth. The biker whipped his head around, his eyes wide.

"You cheap-ass fat fuck," he whispered as his intestines spilled to the ground with wet plops. He dropped to his knees and fell face first into the parking lot's gravel.

Koloth turned his attention to the store and saw a large monster rising up from the rubble. The thing was at least fifty feet tall. It stood on short, squat hind legs and had long muscular ape-like arms. The thing's body grotesquely bulged like a steroid addict with muscles covered in tight dark brown leather-like skin. Its head was forced down low from a hunchback, and it regarded them with pitch-black dinner plate sized eyes. It roared through a massive mouth of giant sharp teeth, each the size of a broadsword.

"What the fuck is that thing?" yelled the biker with meth sores.

It's a Rancor thought Koloth.

The beast roared again and rushed forward. Each step shook the parking lot.

"Fuck," screamed the pierced biker. "Don't just look at it, shoot it!" He pulled out a handgun and began to fire at the monster. The other bikers followed suit. The air was filled with deafening blare of gun fire and the sulphury stench of gun powder.

If the bullets hurt the beast at all, it didn't show. Within moments, it descended upon them.

The monster picked up the pierced biker by the legs while the other bikers scattered around firing more shots. The pierced biker screamed and the beast shook him in the air and then slammed him hard against the pavement, his head exploding like a pumpkin with a firecracker inside.

The beast tossed the corpse aside and snatched up Koloth around his waist. It held him up high in the air and roared.

"Come at me, beast," challenged Koloth and he waved the bat'leth in front of himself. He held it firmly with both hands and was ready for a fight.

The beast looked at him with blank, dead eyes and then tossed Koloth in its mouth. Koloth screamed as he was tossed, head first, straight down the monster's throat. He had his bat'leth pointed forward as he was swallowed whole. The beast's mouth stank like garbage. The Klingon weapon sliced the monster's throat from the inside and Koloth went flowing into its belly along with waves of blood.

The bikers watched it eat the fat nerd and the beast turned to look at them. They fired off more shots and the beast made like it was about to pounce again but then it suddenly went still. It stood up straight and started to jerk about. It opened its mouth and instead of another roar, blood poured out. Its human-like hands grasped its neck and its eyes bulged.

Then it suddenly went still and toppled on its side.

"What the fuck happened?" asked Freebase.

"I don't know. Fucker looks dead," said the mohawked biker.

"Yo, check out its belly," said the biker with the meth sores.

The monster was completely still and obviously dead but there was movement in its abdomen. Not like it was breathing but like something was trying to get out. The stomach jutted forward and back, out and back in. Each time it went out, it was further and further until, finally, Koloth's bat'leth tore its way through.

The blade slid out and down, cutting a several-foot-wide hole in the beast's belly. Koloth fell out covered in gore, along with several internal organs.

He slammed to the ground, coughing, and rubbing the stinging stomach acids from his eyes. He looked up and saw the bikers standing in a circle around him.

Koloth leapt to his feet and held out the bat'leth to the bikers.

"Come on then," said Koloth. He coughed up some of the monster's blood he had swallowed on his way out.

They were silent. Stunned. They stood in front of him looking back and forth between their leader's disemboweled corpse, the dead monster, each other, and Koloth.

Finally the mohawked biker spoke up, addressing Koloth.

"So boss, what now?"

Koloth breathed heavily and wiped the blood from his face with the back of his hand. He sighed and slumped his shoulders with relief when he saw the bikers putting away their guns.

He observed his new followers and smiled.

"We got to get you all a new look. Something . . . something more honorable."

17
WHO WOULD WIN IN A FIGHT, STEAMPUNKS OR KLINGONS?

The Klingon bikers screamed with blood lust. They paired up and created giant slingshots by stretching long strips of rubber between them. A third biker loaded something small into each slingshot and lit it on fire.

Four small flaming balls flew through the air, high up and over the walls. The balls squealed loudly as they soared over their heads.

"Well what pray tell is that," said Brunkshire.

Three of them landed harmlessly amongst the people below, they scattered and no one appeared injured. One, however, landed on the roof of one of the buildings. It wiggled around and the fire slowly started to spread.

"The brutes have set our haberdashery aflame," said Brunkshire. He shouted down at a group of steampunkers on the ground below. "The roof of fourteenth and Bakersfield is aflame. Be quick to it."

The bikers loaded up another round and fired again. One of the shots fell very short and landed on the lookout right between Benny, Gary, Janice, and Brunkshire. It was a small ball, just bigger than a softball. It wiggled around and squealed in pain.

Gary stomped down on it. And then stomped down again and again until the fire went out and it stopped wiggling.

"Fucking bastards are throwing flaming tribbles at us," said Gary.

Another volley came over the walls and then another. Several of the buildings right inside the gate were beginning to burn. People below scurried to attend to the fires.

Brunkshire watched the fires catch. "Savages," he muttered. He turned to the Klingon bikers and screamed, "Savages!"

One of the bikers shot forward from the pack from down

on the far end. He rode along the wall tight and close. As he passed the front gate, he tossed something small and black at the gates and made a sharp turn back to the group.

"Oh fuck," said Benny seeing what was thrown.

The grenade went off and the gates blew inward spewing deadly sharp splinters. Many of the steampunkers were gathered there prepared to take on their attackers, when the explosion happened. The force shattered the bones, brains, and bodies of those closest. The people behind were impaled by rocketing chunks of wood.

Brunkshire saw his people maimed and killed. For a moment he was frozen at the sight of the carnage. His face read horror and sorrow. But he quickly regained his composure, in the most British way possible, and addressed his people.

"Ready your arms. This is the time our Clockwork saviors spoke of, we must defend ourselves and our paradise!"

Benny grabbed Gary and Janice and pulled them close. He spoke in a hushed voice.

"They got guns and grenades and these stupid fuckers are going to go at them with swords. We've got to get out of here."

Gary and Janice nodded, wide-eyed. They climbed down a ladder against the scaffolding while Brunkshire screamed obscenities at the Klingon bikers.

When they reached the ground, the bikers came pouring in.

The steampunkers, for all their credit, had composed themselves and were waiting by the blown open gates. They completely blocked the entry and stood ten deep with swords drawn. But their defensive formations didn't matter when the first wave of bikers drove past and blasted their shotguns. The first line of people immediately fell, instantly dead or screaming and clutching their stomachs, chests, or faces.

The steampunkers behind looked at each other with doubt. This was two assaults that they lost without the bikers even losing one. They thought they were ready for something like this. Their faith and the clockwork man and woman told them they would be able to defend themselves at the final battle. But it had always just been costumers in the past. If any of them were in a fight in the past, it was on the losing side.

But then bikers came pouring in and it was too late for any self-doubt. They rode their motorcycles straight into the steampunkers, the tires tearing through flesh and their guns wildly blasting.

Benny, Gary, and Janice ran around the back of the crowd and away from the gunfire. They weren't the only ones fleeing. The steampunkers quickly realized that this was a hopeless battle, as half of those defending the gate fell immediately.

More flaming tribbles flew screaming overhead as another wave of Klingon Bikers came rushing in.

Most of the community was deeper in the fort and was not aware of the severity of the attack. They were throughout the compound guarding the various buildings or just milling about waiting for further directions. When they drew their weapons they were confident and strong, but hearing the gunshots and seeing their fellow steampunkers running past caused pangs of fear.

The bikers tore through the compound, shooting at anyone that even moved. A few tried to fight back and defend their fellow steampunks by charging with swords drawn. They were shot down instantly.

Soon the bikers were abandoning their rides and just setting out on foot. Any men they caught were shot in the face and the woman were grabbed, beaten, and stripped. Within minutes the air was filled with the wails of dying men and the screams of violated women.

Benny, with Squishy still peeking out of his satchel, Gary and Janice were running away from the massacre. So far they had managed to stay ahead of the attackers.

At the other end of the compound was another explosion. There was another group of bikers launching an attack from behind. They could hear the roar of more motorcycles pouring in and the screams of those being attacked.

They stopped and turned, running between two of the

wooden buildings. They turned a corner and stopped. The wall in front of them was thirty feet tall with no way up or out. All that was back here was the back of the compound buildings.

Smoke wisped through the air as the tribble fires continued to spread.

"We need to get to the van," said Gary.

"No way," said Janice. "It's back by the front. You want to go there?"

There was a loud roar as a bike came around the corner two buildings down. The rider wore dark black glasses and his blood-splattered face wore a huge, maniacal smile.

They turned to run and another bike came around a building in the other direction.

The only way to go was back the way they came, into the thick of the battle.

With no choice they ran as the engines of the bikes let them know how much closer their death was getting.

The street was in chaos. Just a half an hour ago it was a busy town in the middle of a wasteland. Now, it was burning out of control. A thin stream of blood ran down the street. In every corner a biker was butchering or raping one of the community members. They hadn't even stood a chance.

Two bikers came zooming up the alley behind them and skidded to a stop. The two bikers got off their rides and grinned at Benny, Gary, and Janice.

One of them detached a walkie talkie that was hooked onto his leather vest and spoke into it, "Hey boss, we got 'em."

Both of the bikers raised their guns at them.

They were trapped in the middle of the street with nowhere to go. By the front gate, one of the first buildings to be set on fire collapsed with a boom. Flames and debris shot into the air. The air became thicker with smoke and screams.

And then they saw him.

Koloth came confidently marching out of the smoke. He marched like a Nazi, a huge grin plastered on his face while surveying the carnage. In one hand he held his bat'leth and in the other hand he held the severed head of Brunkshire, the stump still dripping fresh blood to the ground. He stopped a few feet from them and tossed the head to the ground. The two bikers moved to flank him, never taking their guns off of Benny, Gary, or Janice.

"I told you you wouldn't get away," said Koloth, his grin widening to madness proportions.

"Dude, you don't have to do any of this," said Gary.

"He's right," said Benny, backing him up. "Think of all the *Magic* tournaments. Think of all the arguments over the New 52. I get it. You have your own thing going now and you need the town's supplies. Just take everything here and let us go on. For old time's sake."

Benny felt a twang of guilt at what he said about the steampunkers but they were all done for anyway. Their only hope of getting out of this alive was to play at their history with Koloth.

And then that hope was dashed.

Koloth spit on the ground and bared his teeth. He locked eyes with Janice. "Kill them all," he ordered. "Except the girl. I want her."

It was then that Squishy wiggled out of Benny's satchel and ran. Benny tried to grab her but she found the agility and speed from her kitten days to wiggle free.

"Squishy," he yelled, but she flattened her ears and charged forward. She had no concern for herself; she had one goal—to save her humans. And one thought in her little furry head.

Fuck you, Fat Man.

She dashed between Koloth's legs and ran past the other bikers. Nearby their standoff was a small pile of burning rubble that had fallen off of a burning building and Squishy ran straight into it. She crouched down and let the flames lick at her fur.

"Squishy!" Benny, Janice and Gary shouted in unison.

A biker with a green mohawk and holding a length of chain ran up to her. He whipped it back but Squishy stood up on her back legs, extended her claws, and swatted at the air. It was then the flames finally took to her and her long fur and little red uniform went up in bright orange flames. While burning she swatted her front paws in the air at the biker.

He paused in mid-swing and stepped back. Squishy, on her hind legs was at best sixteen inches tall and her paw swats were missing by at least three feet, but this fucking cat was on fire. That's intimidating.

Squishy roared, at least she let out a mew that was the best a housecat could do for a roar, and she ran away from the battle. The bikers, along with Benny, Gary, and Janice diverted their attention and watch the flaming cat scurrying away. As she ran, she was yelping and squeaking in pain from the flames burning away her fur and flesh.

She didn't stop. She kept running, to the building two doors down, the one with all the gasoline drums. The wooden doors were still latched, but there was a gap between the door and the ground of a few inches. It was just enough space. Flaming Squishy wiggled her way under the door and disappeared.

The Klingon bikers turned their attention back to Benny, Gary, and Janice. Their chains, knives, and pipes ready. Gary and Janice saw the shift in attention but Benny was blind to them. His mind was stunned. He had just watched his cat set herself on fire and run into a building filled with gasoline. Then it clicked.

Holy fuck, my cat just set herself on fire and ran into a building full of gasoline!

He turned around to Gary and Janice. "Get down!"

He grabbed them and threw them to the ground and the building exploded. The entire world shook as a wave of heat overtook them all. Everything went bright red and then white and then black.

***

At first, Benny could only see the color grey. His vision blurred and then color and focus began to come back. He was sprawled out and face down. He pushed himself up to look around and he coughed up dirt.

The compound was devastated. Every building had been

blown apart from the explosion or was a raging inferno. The fighting had stopped. Bikers and steampunkers alike wandered the battlefield, looking for friends or just stumbling with vacant stares.

Then Gary's face appeared in front of him. His lips were moving but Benny heard nothing. It was then he became aware of the overwhelming ringing in his ears.

Like a film coming into focus, the world snapped back into place with proper sight and sound.

"Dude, dude. Are you okay?" asked Gary.

"Yeah," said Benny holding his head. "I think so. Janice?" He looked around and saw that she was sitting just to his left. She was coughing and wiping sand from her face and dusting it out of her hair.

"She's fine," confirmed Gary. "Me too, thanks for asking." He turned from Benny and looked around what was left of the compound. "I think we are some of the lucky ones."

Benny stood up and his whole body ached but nothing seemed broken. He walked over to Janice and helped her to her feet.

Koloth was nowhere to be seen but neither were the other two bikers that flanked him. In their place were black pieces of burned fabric and red, fleshy smears.

"Squishy," Benny called out. "Squishy!"

He stumbled in the direction of the building where she had disappeared. Now it was just a scorched crater.

Gary and Janice exchanged a look of concern for their friend.

"Squishy," Benny called out again. He searched through a pile of burnt wooden debris. "Squishy!"

Gary came up behind him, "Benny—"

"Help me find Squishy, she's got to be around here," Benny said through tear-filled eyes. His voice cracked.

Benny went to another pile of rubble and tossed over a board on top. Beneath it was a charred human arm. He turned and called for his cat again.

"Benny," Janice came walking over. "I . . . I don't think Squishy made it."

Benny froze and then turned to her.

"She had to," he said, his voice small and weak.

Gary walked over to him, "I'm sorry man."

"My Squishy . . ."

"She was a good cat," said Janice.

"She was a fucking badass cat," agreed Gary.

Benny nodded and dug around in his pockets for his cigarettes and lit one up.

"Let's get going," said Janice and she put her hand on Benny's shoulder.

He looked around the devastation hoping for some miracle, wishing that his fat cat would come climbing out of the ruins. But all that remained was burning rubble, broken bodies, and the lucky few survivors wandering the devastation.

They walked towards the front grates, where they had left their van.

"I'll be damned," said Gary walking up to the van. "She made it through alright."

"Outside of burn marks and bullet holes, it looks okay," said Janice walking around their vehicle and inspecting it. "Nothing important seems to have been damaged.

"Shall we go?" asked Gary.

Gary and Janice looked to Benny who was just staring off into the sky. His eyes were puffy and he looked to be mentally very far away.

"I'll take the first driving shift," said Janice and she got behind the wheel.

Gary walked over to Benny.

"Come on, man. It's time to go."

A look of surprise flashed across Benny's face when Gary spoke to him and then he regained his composure. Benny nodded and they got in the van.

Janice started the vehicle and slowly pulled through the blasted apart front gates. It was an hour on the dirt road to the highway, and then just four hours south west to Los Angeles and the end of the journey.

PART 3

LET THAT BE YOUR LAST BATTLEFIELD

18
THE DEALER'S TABLE AT THE END OF THE WORLD

They had only been on the highway for about two hours when Benny pulled over into a highway rest stop. It was just a large patch of dirt with a small bathroom in the center.

The three of them got out of the van and Benny lit up a smoke.

"What's up?" asked Gary.

Benny didn't reply.

"Yo man," said Gary trying again. "Why'd we stop? We only got, like, another two hours and then we're in LaLa-Land and we can save the Shat."

"Oh fuck Shatner and fuck your stupid ass plan," said Benny turning to Gary. "I can't believe I let myself actually go along with this."

"Fuck Shatner . . ." repeated Gary in disbelief.

"Yeah, and fuck you too."

"Dude calm—"

"No. This was pointless and stupid from the beginning. And now my cat is gone. My Squishy . . ." his voice got quiet at the end.

"Benny, it will be OK," said Janice trying to comfort him.

"And what the hell makes you think that? How are we even going to find Shatner when we get there? Fuck, odds are he's already fucking dead. Everyone is fucking dead and we will be soon at this rate."

"So what do you propose then?" responded Gary. "That we just turn back? We're almost to L.A. as it is."

"I don't know," said Benny. "We could just head to the ocean. Live on the beach until zombies or marauders kill us. Besides, even if we do get to Shatner, how could we save him? We've barely been able to take care of ourselves."

"Self-doubt is always the bane of the thinking person," said a highly cultured voice from behind them.

They spun around, surprised. Behind them, where before had just been an empty dirt parking lot, were now three folding tables covered with an array of books, DVDs, and toys. Behind the table was a tall man wearing a three piece bright purple suit with a bright pink tie. He had neatly cropped hair and a long pointed goatee.

"It is key not to let our own fears get the best of us," he said and smiled.

"Whoa dude," said Gary. "Where the hell did you come from?"

"I've always been here and I suspect I always will be. These are my goods. I think it would be more appropriate for me to ask you where you came from but I must admit that it concerns me little."

Benny, Gary, and Janice each took a step back.

The man chuckled. "Now now, there is no need for concern. I understand your trepidation in these strange days but I am neither threat nor foe. Just a humble merchant with his goods." He waved his hands at the tables. "Come, have a look, perhaps I have something that you desire. Besides, if I were a danger, surely you would know by now."

They looked at each other and walked cautiously to the tables. They were almost overflowing with items. A quick glance over them revealed that all the books, DVDs, and various collectibles were all related to science-fiction, fantasy, and horror.

Janice picked up one of the DVDs. "I didn't know Jodorowsky made an adaptation of *Dune*."

"He didn't," said Gary and taking the DVD from her. He studied the cover and flipped it over to read the back. "Music by Pink Floyd, staring Orson Welles and Salvador Dali? This movie was supposed to get made, in the seventies, but it never did. This is impossible."

"How about *At the Mountains of Madness* directed by Guillermo del Toro starring Tom Cruise?" said Benny holding up another DVD.

Gary snatched it out of his hands.

"That was another one that never got made. These can't be real."

"Oh sir," spoke up the vendor. "I can assure you that they are indeed real. Bootlegs, true. But they are, shall we say, the real deal."

"Where did these come from?" asked Gary.

"I have my suppliers . . . they can get their hands on rather . . . uncommon items."

"Wow," said Benny while holding up a caped action figure. "Anarky from Batman."

"Volume three of *Howard the Duck* by Steve Gerber."

"Do you have a TV?" asked Gary.

"I'm sorry to say I do not. My customers must provide their own way of . . . experiencing my wears." The man held out his hands apologetically. He lifted his head and his face broadened in a huge smile. "But I do have something that I suspect you will find of great interest."

He reached underneath the table and pulled out a small shiny silver ball. He held it out to them.

"What is that?" asked Gary. "It looks like a mini disco ball."

He took it from the vendor and held it in his hands. He rolled it around and he could swear that there was a faint pulse from it. Not like a heartbeat, something groovier.

"No thanks," he said handing it back.

"But why not? This could be your deus ex machina moment. You've read "The Monkey's Paw," or at least seen *The Simpsons* episode. You've seen *Hellraiser*. View me as another plot device, another step towards the end of your journey."

"What the fuck's that supposed to mean," said Gary. "How do you know we're headed somewhere?"

The man smiled and guested around the barren landscape, "I assume this is neither the end of your journey or your story." He turned his head and looked west. "But the coast is not far so I suspect one or the other may be ending soon."

"If we're supposed to be interested in it, what do you want for it?" asked Benny.

"It's already yours. It was always yours," he said and bowed his head. The air suddenly blew hard and fierce, whipping sand around. Benny, Gary, and Janice had to shield their eyes and the dust storm picked up even more strength. It whipped around them and everyone went brown, blinding them all.

Just as quickly as it all started, it became calm and still again—the sand falling to the ground. They uncovered their eyes and looked around but the dealer was now gone. Where the stand of books and movies had mysteriously appeared, it had just as mysteriously vanished.

Benny looked down and was surprised to find that he was holding the small disco ball. He glanced over at Janice and Gary, who looked just as confused as him.

"What the hell was that all about?" said Janice breaking the silence.

"I have no idea," said Benny rolling the small softball sized disco ball in his hands. The pulse he thought he felt before was now gone.

Benny tapped the ball with his finger and it sounded like hard plastic.

"*It was always yours*," said Janice quoting the strange man.

"Why do you think he wanted you to have it?" asked Gary.

"I have no idea."

"Fuck," Gary kicked at the dirt. "I wish I would have grabbed some of those figures before he disappeared."

Benny ignored him. "He also said our journey was almost over . . ."

"That's some cryptic shit there," said Janice. "Those movies he mentioned, the stories didn't end too well for any of the characters. You think that's what he meant about us?"

Benny and Gary didn't answer her question.

Gary shook his head, "I fucking hate this apocalypse." He turned to Benny. "So, what now?"

Benny turned and faced in the direction of Los Angeles. The warm air whipped against his face and the small disco ball seemed to be getting warmer in his hands, just ever so slightly.

"I think it's time to hit the road." He turned to Gary and Janice and smiled. "We're almost there."

19
L.A.'S BURNING

They passed the mini disco ball around in the car but there was no clue as to why the strange man had given it to them.

"Where should we go to first?" asked Janice.

"Shatner's got a place in Beverly Hills. We should check it out there," said Gary.

"What makes you think he'd be at home when all the shit hit the fan? What if he was at a studio filming something or a press event?"

"I already told you. He posted on twitter that he was doing his cameo shots for the second *Star Trek* remake. The shots were happening while we were at the con and they were scheduled for two more weeks. He would have been in L.A."

"I still think it's a little creepy that you know that," said Janice.

"But what makes you think we should try his place or that he'd stay in L.A.?" asked Benny.

"Because he's a rich celebrity. They all have panic rooms and that kind of shit. He'd be holed up there, wouldn't you?"

Benny shrugged, there was a logic to his argument.

"And if he's not there," continued Gary, "we zip over to Paramount Studios. Guys, we can do this."

"I'm still not so sure he's not dead," said Benny.

"Oh, he's not," said Gary. "I know it."

They kept driving and saw the smoke before they saw the city. Rising over the horizon thick torrents of black belched into the sky.

"You think that's L.A.?" asked Janice.

"My guess is yes," said Benny.

As they neared the city, the fires became more apparent. Buildings came into view and the devastation was widespread.

The highway took them around the edge of the city. Most of it was already in ruins. Houses caved in and tall office buildings lay in ruins on their side. The other side of the highway, leading out of the city, was jammed with a solid gridlock of abandoned cars. Leading into the city, they were the only vehicle in sight.

"What do you think happened here?" asked Janice.

Benny shook his head. "Could be anything. A lot of strange stuff has been happening these days. But more importantly, any idea how we get to Shatner's?"

"Yeah," said Gary. "Stay on the highway until the signs direct us to Beverly Hills. Then we should try to find one of those maps of movie star homes. Should be a cinch."

They drove and, just like Gary said, an exit for Beverly Hills came up. Benny took it and soon they were in a posh residential neighborhood. Or what used to be one.

Most of the houses were in ruins and bodies littered the streets and yards. Benny stopped the car at the highway off-ramp's stop sign, there were no other cars coming but it was force of habit. In the intersection directly in front of them was a corpse, several days old from the looks of it. The withered body was wrapped tight in a short red dress and in her stick-like arms was a dead Chihuahua. Her dress was torn open at the stomach and someone or something had disemboweled her and shoved an Xbox inside her abdomen.

"Which way?" asked Benny.

Gary leaned forward from the back seat and looked around. "Pick a direction. We're looking for any gas station or convenience store or something like that. They'll have one of those maps."

Benny drove around the corpse and headed straight.

It looked like a bomb had gone off in the neighborhood. Debris and bodies littered the streets and Benny had to drive slowly to avoid all the obstacles. They had only gone a block when they saw the first Zombie Borg. It was leaning over a ruined, upside-down pickup truck, pulling out cables and wires from the undercarriage and shoving them into its body.

Benny drove the car around the Zombie Borg and they

all held their breath, hoping it wouldn't notice them.

It jerked its head and turned to appraise them as they went by but it was not interested and went back to the truck parts and continued to mangle itself.

"They're even here," said Janice once they were past.

"Yo," Gary shouted and pointed. "Over there."

At the next street corner was a gas station. They pulled into the parking lot and got out. It was one of those huge corporate gas stations that also doubled as a mini-mart.

They approached the building and it looked in surprisingly good shape. Whatever had torn through the area had missed it. They walked inside.

"Damn," said Benny looking around the store.

The shelves were all knocked over and barren. It had long ago been raided.

"I was hoping we'd be able to get a snack," said Janice as she walked through the debris of upended shelves and empty soda bottles and potato chip bags.

"Stay focused," said Gary as he rushed to the check-out counter.

Benny looked back out the doors but didn't see any threats coming. Except for the smell of smoke in the air, it was a nice sunny day. The stillness and quiet would have been calming had they not been in a major American city.

"Boo-fuckin'-yeah," shouted Gary and he held up a folded pamphlet.

"You found it?" said Janice.

"Yep," replied Gary as he unfolded the map and studied it. "Just got to find Shatner in the directory on the back here . . . yeah, there he is." Gary flipped the map over and ran his finger along searching. "Boom! Right there." He poked the map hard. "It looks like we're only about a mile or two away."

He looked up at Benny, a huge smile on his face. "Let's get going to William Shatner's house."

***

The driving was slow, and they saw more dead bodies and fallen debris, but soon they were out of the thick urban sprawl and driving up the hillside. The buildings changed from small houses and businesses to large mansions.

"Okay," said Gary directing from the backseat. "Take a right up there and the next left."

Benny did and slowly went up the street.

"Okay . . . okay, it should be one of these," said Gary scanning the mail-box numbers. "There, there it is, 737."

Benny turned into the driveway and they drove up a steep incline around the corner of the hill. There, snuggled back into the trees, was a large white mansion.

"This is Shatner's place?" asked Janice.

"That's what the map says." The excitement was audible in Gary's voice.

Benny parked the car in front of the house and they all got out. Gary ran up the steps to the front porch.

"Are we sure this is the right place?" Benny asked looking around, as he and Janice walked up steps.

"I think so," beamed Gary. He pointed above the front door to a porcelain bust of William Shatner stoically looking down at them.

"So what should we do?" asked Benny, a little amazed they actually made it here.

Gary shrugged and pushed the doorbell. They could hear the customized bell-ring of an audience applauding but there was no answer or any sound of movement from inside.

"Should we break in?" asked Benny.

"Shatner might shoot us," said Gary.

"Shatner's into guns?"

"Hey guys . . ." Janice said.

"Fuck yeah. Remember *Boston Legal*? That scene where he pulls out all the concealed guns? That's why the Republicans wanted him to run for president."

"Guys . . ." said Janice again.

"Denny Crane isn't real. He was just acting."

"How can you be sure?"

"Guys, shut the fuck up," shouted Janice. "Look."

They turned and saw she had walked off the porch and was pointing away from the house. They were high up on the mountain side and could see for miles over the entire sprawled out city. The fires raged freely and the devastation was immense.

"What the hell?" said Benny once he saw what had attracted her attention.

About half a mile away in the distance, a giant man, hundreds of feet tall, was tearing a house from its foundation. He pulled it out of the ground and tossed it through the air. The building flew like a cheap toy and smashed to the street.

The giant roared with delight at the destruction. The huge man had grey hair, was a bit paunchy, and was wearing torn up khaki pants and a blue button-up dress shirt.

There was a vague twinge of recognition at the man and his voice.

"Wait, wait, dudes is that . . ." Gary trailed off.

"Yeah," Benny said. "It is."

"Oh god . . ." moaned Janice.

"Well," said Benny. "We found William Shatner."

20
WILLIAM SHATNER'S STORY

"I'm really honored that you granted us this interview, Mr. Shatner."

William Shatner smiled and nodded and took a sip of his wine. He was sitting with a skinny young guy, in his early thirties at the latest. He had thick glasses and neatly cropped hair. He dressed like an IT guy.

Dear god, back to this again, thought Shatner.

"It's really exciting to see you back on the big screen after taking a couple years off. Your fans haven't seen anything from William Shatner in just over four years."

"Yes . . . I had some . . . things . . . to deal with . . . but I'm ready again . . . ready to get . . . back in front of . . . the public."

"It's interesting to see you coming back in the new *Star Trek*. For decades you seemed to avoid your association with the franchise—pursuing critically acclaimed runs on *Boston Legal* and a surprisingly experimental and successful music career."

"I . . . consider myself an . . . artist . . . before anything else . . . I . . . have . . . creative wings that I need . . . to spread . . . and soar."

"But why come back to *Star Trek* after all these years?"

Shatner took another sip of his wine.

"My fans . . . have always wanted to see . . . me . . . go back to the . . . character I made . . . iconic . . . now that . . . Chris . . . has his own spin and following on . . . Captain Kirk . . . it . . . just . . . seemed right to . . . pass on the mantle . . . so to say."

"Awesome. I understand that you're going to your first day of filming after our interview. Is there anything you can tell me about the scenes you are in?"

"Haha, no . . . they'd . . . sick the Klingons on me . . . if I . . . spoiled anything."

"Well, this is also an exciting time because this is the first work you've done in four years. Ever since that terrible disaster at ShatnerCon, you've kept a low profile."

"Yes . . . that was a . . . terrible weekend . . . not a day goes by where . . . I . . . don't think of all the people . . . who . . . died because of their . . . love . . . for me."

"Three thousand was the final death toll. Official investigators reported that the terrorists used a combination of gas and explosives. But I have heard the unofficial story is that it was some kind of a fiction bomb that malfunctioned, bringing the fictional characters from your movies to life in the real world. They say that you were responsible for having to kill them off. No one's really been able to figure out what happened that weekend. All we really know is that you were the only survivor."

"I . . . was . . . fortunate."

"Care to address the rumors that the attack was an attempt on your life? And that the reason you've been out of the public spotlight for four years was right after the convention, there was another attempt on your life that caused you to have a nervous breakdown?"

Shatner took and large gulp of wine and emptied the glass.

"No . . . comment."

***

Godamn, I hate that fucking pandering.

Shatner hurried down the street. The nineteen bus was supposed to arrive in three minutes and he still had two blocks to go.

He jogged down the street, panting and sweating.

Shit, this is not how I wanted to show up.

He didn't really want do the new *Star Trek* movie but he was doing it for the same reason that he was rushing to the bus stop, four years of not working had left him broke. He needed money and his agent had at least negotiated a nice paycheck. He tried so hard to get away from that stupid Sci-

Fi show and be regarded as a real actor, but if this is what he had to do to keep food on the table . . .

Sonofabitch, he thought as he turned the corner and saw his bus, a block away, pulling away from the stop.

Fuck, I'm going to be late.

He took out his cell phone and hit the contact button for his agent.

"WE'RE SORRY," said an automated voice through his phone. "THIS ACCOUNT HAS BEEN SUSPENDED DUE TO AN OUTSTANDING BALANCE."

Shatner put his phone in his pocket and looked around.

There was a pay phone on the other side of the street.

Shatner ran across to it, dodging through four lanes of traffic. He reached it and took the receiver off and held it against his ear as he dug through his pockets for change. He dropped the coins in the payphone and looked up the number of his agent on his cell phone.

It rang and then, "hello?"

"Hey . . . Arnie . . . It's Bill."

"Oh hey Bill, what can I do for you?"

"Can you . . . call the studio . . . and tell them . . . I'll . . . be . . . a little late."

There was a pause on the other end.

"Didn't you get my message?"

"What . . . message?"

"I'm sorry Bill, they decided to go with someone else."

"Someone else . . . but . . . I'm . . . Captain Kirk."

"Yeah, and they respect that. They just decided to go with someone else for the role."

"Who?"

"James Doohan."

"Jimmy . . . but . . . he's been dead . . . for years."

"Yeah, but they got this amazing new 3D hologram technology and it will be just like he's really there, it's pretty spectacular. Audiences are going to love it."

"So . . . they . . . don't need me?"

"Not for this one Bill, but don't take it the wrong way. I spoke with J. J. and he totally wants you for one of the sequels. I'll keep talking to . . ."

The agent kept talking but Shatner had stopped listening. He was replaced. By a dead man!

There was some more talk of possible future job offers but nothing specific and nothing about a paycheck and then Shatner hung up.

What am I going to do?

And then *it* happened. In Los Angeles everyone saw a bright, blinding flash and heard the sound of a camera shutter.

Shatner's vision went white and everything gradually came back into focus. He looked around for the paparazzi, at first annoyed and then flattered that someone cared to invade his privacy, but there was no one around.

"Captain, what are your orders?"

He turned around and there were four tall broad shouldered men with chiseled chins, wearing red Star Fleet uniforms. They stood at attention with phasers drawn.

"I'm . . . sorry . . . no autographs," said Shatner turning away.

"Captain," said one of the red shirts. "We've been getting some very strange readings from the tricorders. There has been a massive disruption in the space/time continuum."

"Really," said Shatner turning back to them. "I . . . don't have time . . . for this."

"Captain, we need you," said another red shirt.

The street next to them suddenly exploded, concrete went flying through the air.

A large chunk hit one of the red shirts, sending him flying into a brick wall. He was crushed flat between the two and his body was covered by the massive piece of pavement. A stream of blood began to run out from between the concrete and brick building.

Shatner and the other three red shirts turned in the direction of the explosion to see several massive purple tentacles reaching out from the street. They were as thick as garbage cans and whipped around searching for prey.

"Protect the Captain," shouted one of the red shirts.

The three men in Star Fleet uniforms rushed in front of

Kirk and fired their phasers at the monstrous tentacles. Their guns made the same sound as they did from the show and thin red beams shot from them at the tentacles.

The tentacles twitched when they were hit and an unearthly squeal erupted from somewhere deep underground.

Two of the tentacles darted forward and each snatched up a red shirt.

"Get back," said the third red shirt, pushing William Shatner in the direction of a nearby alley.

"What's . . . happening?"

"No time to explain. Run," yelled the red shirt.

They ran down the alley while the two other crewmen were pulled screaming down underneath the street.

They reached the next street and that's when Shatner took notice of the screams and explosions coming from every direction. He stopped on the sidewalk and looked up and down the street.

Traffic had come to a stand-still and he could see people running in every direction amongst the cars. Somewhere many blocks away, something exploded in the crowd and Shatner saw a small fireball rising into the air.

"Captain," said the red shirt next to him. "We have to find someplace safe. I tried contacting the Enterprise but they're not answering my hails."

"Please," said Shatner. "This . . . is . . . serious . . . your friends . . . might be . . . dead . . . we need . . . to get . . . help."

"Sir I know, our best bet is to contact the ship."

"I . . . can't . . . deal . . . with this right now," said Shatner as he began to hurry away from the obviously deranged man.

"Captain," shouted the red shirt from behind.

"It's . . . just . . . a character," Shatner yelled as he began to run.

The red shirt started to run too. "Captain!"

Shatner ran as fast as his old limbs and clogged arteries would allow. Then someone stepped out in front of him. Whoever they were, they had the body of a brick wall and Shatner crumpled to the sidewalk.

Shatner looked up to see a tall man in a full body Gorn

costume. He wore a brown toga and his exposed muscular arms and legs were covered in green skin. On top of his head was an over-sized lizard-mask with beady eyes and a long snout.

The eyes turned in the mask and a tongue darted out of the mouth.

That's a really good mask.

"Captain, a Gorn."

A really good mask. This can't be happening again . . . things from fiction becoming real . . . another fiction bomb? A fiction nuke?

The red shirt had caught up to them and aimed his phaser at the Gorn. As the red beam blasted out, the lizard-ball started twitching and his body glowed neon crimson. Then his image faded in and out and he disappeared.

"That was close," said the red shirt as he holstered the phaser.

He held out his hand to Shatner. "Come Captain. We must find a way to reach the ship."

Shatner let the man help him to his feet and then he dusted the dirt off his clothes.

"You . . . know . . . I'm not really . . . Captain Kirk."

The red shirt cocked his head and gave his a strange look. "Are you feeling okay, Sir?"

"I . . . think . . . I should be the one . . . asking you that."

"Sir, there's no time to argue. You need help. You need—"

There was the piercing sound of tires screeching and Shatner turned around to see a truck pulling a huge flatbed flipping over in the street just yards away. On the back of the truck were dozens of yellow barrels labeled with black "toxic" symbols.

The barrels smashed open as the truck over turned releasing a wave of thick green goo.

It washed over Shatner and the red shirt and they were both drenched with the substance.

The red shirt started screaming and Shatner looked over to witness the man's clothes and skin dissolving. He shrieked and the bright red muscle beneath began to turn to liquid and run away. He fell to his knees as more of his flesh dripped off his bones and he was little more than just a skeleton with eyeballs. Then the eyes turned to white mush and he fell over.

As this happened, and Shatner watched, he started feeling further and further away from the death. The man's body seemed to get smaller and smaller. Shatner felt his skin tingle. His muscles seemed to stretch. He saw the tops of buildings and then all the way out to the Pacific Ocean.

What's happening to me?

Shatner looked down and realized that he had grown hundreds of feet tall.

He patted his body and he seemed normal, other than his massive height. He was still fully clothed and unharmed in any other way.

He surveyed the landscape and noticed that everyone in the surrounding area was pointing up at him.

Everyone was paying attention to him.

"Captain. Captain," shouted a small voice by his feet.

Shatner looked down to see one of the red shirts from earlier that had been pulled underground by tentacles. His uniform was now all torn up and ragged.

"Captain," he said. "I stopped the beast. Dover . . . wasn't so lucky." The red shirt looked Shatner up and down. "Captain. What happened to you?"

Shatner reached down and picked up the man and held him in front of his huge face. He balled his fist around him with just the red shirt's head sticking out.

"For . . . the . . . last time . . . I'm . . . not . . . the Captain."

He brought the man's head to his mouth and bit down. His teeth cut right through his neck. Shatner spit the head out and it went soaring through the air, crashing through a taxi cab's windshield.

He tossed the corpse away and picked up and a city bus. The commuters inside screamed as Shatner's huge eyes glared in at them. He then threw the bus as hard as he could into a nearby five-story office building.

The building crumbled down, burying the public

transport vehicle in debris.

Shatner turned around and looked over Los Angeles. The city that had made all his dreams and nightmares come true.

There was a loud scream from the ground and Shatner saw a woman fleeing and pushing a baby carriage. Shatner stomped down on them and the screaming stopped.

This was his city now.

21
SHATZILLA, KING OF THE ACTORS

"So William Shatner's turned into a giant and is rampaging across the city," said Janice. "This is unexpected."

"I don't think he needs our saving," said Benny.

Shatner was stomping down again and again on a ranch house. He stopped and leaned over. Even though he was so far away, they could see he was picking up a person. The captive thrashed about in his massive hands.

Shatner laughed and the noise bellowed across the valley.

He pinched one of the person's arms between his thumb and index finger and plucked it off like a cruel child would to a fly's wings. He laughed again and pulled off the other arm and then the person's legs. Shatner looked down at the torso in his hand, laughed again, and tossed it over his shoulder.

They could see the small shape of the poor victim fly through the air and to the ground somewhere in the distance.

"Well fuck," said Benny.

Suddenly Shatner whipped his head around and he was staring straight at them.

"Who's . . . at . . . my home," he yelled and the words echoed.

He ran in the direction of the hill-top. His giant stride leaping blocks at a time and his body slamming through what structures were still standing. Each footfall shook the earth. *BOOM. BOOM. BOOM.*

Benny began backing up towards the van, unable to tear his eyes away. "I think we need to go."

Janice was back-peddling and nodded.

The two of them turned to the van and bolted. They reached it and hopped in but Gary wasn't with them.

Benny rolled down the window. "Gary, come on!"

Gary smiled back at them. "Guys don't worry. I got this."

Then he turned back to the oncoming giant William Shatner.

"He's lost it," said Janice.

Gary held out his arms and smiled at his oncoming hero.

Shatner was now practically on top of them. They were on the side of a steep hill so even though he was only a few dozen yards away, his face was level with them. Seeing how outrageously huge he was took their breath away for a moment.

"Gary!" yelled Janice from the van.

He ignored her and stared straight into the truck tire sized eyes of the man who had gotten him through the roughest times in his life.

Shatner cocked his head and glared down at Gary. "Who . . . are you?"

"Yo, it's me. We finally got here. It's so exciting to finally be meeting you face to face," said Gary. "I brought my friends. We're here to save you."

Shatner looked at him like he was an idiot. "Save . . . me?"

"Yeah, we finally made it. Dude, we couldn't have done it without you. That was really smooth back there with those zombies."

Shatner raised a giant eyebrow.

"So you called, dude, I'm here," Gary grinned up at his idol

"What?"

"You said you'd need me? Here I am."

Shatner gritted his teeth. "You . . . crazy nerd . . . get . . . a life."

Shatner raised his huge fist and brought it down. Gary leapt to the side and narrowly avoided the boulder sized hand that would have squashed him. The fist hit the ground with such force that it still knocked him over.

"Dude, what the fuck? It's me, Gary," he said while standing up.

"Gary," yelled Benny from the van as he started it, "get back here."

Shatner raised his fist again and Gary turned and ran. The fist crashed to the ground next to him narrowly missing him by just a few feet.

Gary reached the van and jumped in the back seat. "Go, go," he shouted.

"What the fuck was all that?" shouted Janice.

"Just go," yelled Gary.

Benny put the van in drive and slammed on the gas. The wheels screamed and the van took off down the drive way.

Behind them, William Shatner was climbing up the hilltop and reaching for them. Gary looked out the back window as the giant ran in pursuit.

The van hit the main road and Shatner lunged to grab it. Benny made a hard left and the giant just missed them. He stumbled from his own force and crashed into a mansion on the other side of the street.

"I think that was Edward Norton's place," said Gary as he took out the star-map.

"Never mind that," yelled Janice at him.

Benny tore down the street as Shatner stood up.

"You . . . can't escape me," he yelled and ran after them.

"Go faster, go faster," said Gary.

"I'm doing the best I can," said Benny as he swerved through the road trying to avoid scattered building debris, huge potholes, and old corpses.

"He's almost on top of us," said Janice.

Shatner's huge stride and ability to just walk through any obstacles did indeed have him almost on top of them.

He swiped at the van and Benny jerked to the right and sped down a side street. Shatner lurched straight through a two-story apartment building raining down concrete and wood.

Benny slammed the van left, down another street, and gave it more gas. They sped down the straight road while Shatner stumbled through the buildings, momentarily slowed.

"That's it, keep going," said Gary but the van started to slow. "What are you—?"

He turned to see that the road ahead was blocked with two dozen Zombie Borg. They were standing in two straight lines across the lanes.

151

"Go through them," said Janice.

"The van could get fucked up," said Benny.

"It's better than what's coming," shouted Gary. "Fucking go!"

Benny sped up the van.

"RESISTANCE IS FUTILE," said the Borg in unison.

The van hit them and shook and bounced and three were sucked beneath the tires. One flew over the hood and slammed, head-first into the windshield. The glass cracked and was splattered with blood and brains. Then they were through them and headed down the street.

Shatner reached the Zombie Borg and stopped. He looked down at them and they looked up at him.

"YOUR BIOLOGICAL AND TECHNOLOGICAL—"

Shatner stomped down onto three of the Zombie Borg. Their bodies were immediately reduced to crumpled metal and smooshed flesh. Shatner smashed down again, taking another two of them.

He reached down and picked up one of the Zombie Borg and threw it as hard as he could into the air. The reanimated body flew through the air into the distance.

"The Gorn . . . were better," the giant bellowed.

22

WHAT TO DO
IN CASE OF A GIANT
WILLIAM SHATNER ATTACK

"What the hell are you doing?" shouted Janice. "Keep going."

"No," said Benny. "Just get down and stay quiet."

Benny pulled the van into a small alleyway between two burnt out apartment buildings and turned off the engine.

He crouched down in the seat and looked back towards the road. The buildings on both sides of them obscured the view on both sides. They could only see the roads immediately in front and behind them.

Janice and Gary exchanged nervous looks and then crouched down following Benny's example.

"There's no way we could out-run him," whispered Benny. "We have to lose him."

They were silent and everything seemed still for a minute and then they heard and felt the *BOOM BOOM* of Shatner's steps.

"I guess he's done with them," said Gary.

Janice shushed him.

The road behind them suddenly went dark as a giant shadow fell across it. Then they could see the huge loafer of William Shatner step down into view. As the huge foot landed, the whole car bounced.

"Where . . . where...are you?" said Shatner as he kept walking.

Then the leg was gone and the booming footsteps were moving away from them.

They were silent for at least another five minutes, until they could hear no sign of Shatner.

"I think we're okay," said Benny.

He got out of the car and fumbled for his cigarettes. With shaking hands he lit up.

Janice and Gary nervously got out of the car. Benny took a deep drag and then slowly walked to the edge of the alley. He peeked around the corner and his body relaxed.

"We're okay," he said, "I don't see him."

He turned and walked around to his friends.

"Well what the fuck was that all about?" said Janice.

"William Shatner just tried to kill us," said Benny.

Gary was pacing. "This just doesn't make any sense."

"Are you okay?" asked Janice. "He almost got you back there."

Gary looked at her and she could see he was trying to hold back tears. He sniffed. "Yeah, I'm okay."

"What was all that shit you were talking?" said Benny. "You were acting like you knew him."

"I do," said Gary.

Benny and Janice looked at each other.

"No, you don't," said Janice.

"Yeah," Gary said, "I do.

"Well," said Benny, "doesn't look like Shatner needs our help."

"Of course he does," shouted Gary. "Something's obviously happened to him. We need to help him get back to normal."

Benny shook his head, "We need to get out of here and save ourselves. He didn't seem too happy to see us."

"Come on, we came all this way to save William Shatner, he needs our help. He needs my help."

"Man, you're crazy."

"I am not crazy," screamed Gary through tears. "We have to help him. He helped me. He helped *us*. He was the one that got us out of the convention."

"No," said Janice, "you led the way and got us out of the convention."

"*He* told me, through the TV! How do you think I knew where the exit was? Or with those crazy cultists? Shatner was there for us."

"What do you mean, 'through the TV?'" asked Benny.

"He speaks to me through TV. Ever since my second

OD. Shatner's been talking to me. I know everyone else is just seeing the shows, but when Shatner's on the screen he's talking to me. Like, literally, talking to me. He's been giving me advice and help for years."

Benny and Janice didn't know what to say.

"That's why I wanted to come," said Gary. "He's always been there for me, I wanted to be there for him."

"Are you saying Squishy died because of your delusions?" said Benny.

"No," said Gary. "Squishy saved us. Just like Shatner did. You saved Squishy once, now's my chance to save someone."

"How long has Shatner been talking to you?" asked Janice.

"After my relapse," said Gary.

Benny and Janice skeptically looked at him.

"I know how that sounds," said Gary. "But you have to believe me. He's been asking for my help."

"Gary," Benny said gently, "I'm not sure what you've been seeing but the William Shatner we just met has been leveling L.A. and just tried to kill us."

Gary went to speak but he couldn't think of how to respond.

"He's right," said Janice. "We have to save ourselves."

Gary looked at the two of them, his mouth agape, and then looked down.

"We're your friends," said Benny. "Your real friends, the ones that have been there for you through all of this."

Gary stayed silent.

"Hold on," said Janice, "does anyone else hear music?"

Benny and Gary listened. They too could hear what sounded like the muffled rhythm of music from somewhere close.

It seemed to be coming from the van. Benny looked at Janice and Gary and walked over to it. As he got closer it got louder and louder until he was right next to the car and it suddenly went quiet.

He looked in through the window and on the back seat

was the mini disco ball. It was now pulsing with light. Each time it lit up and went out it changed color. Red, green, blue, purple, and more—all the colors of the rainbow.

He reached in and picked it up. It seemed to hum with energy.

"What's going on?" asked Gary.

"I'm not sure," said Benny walking over and cradling the ball in his hands.

The ball started flashing the lights and colors again, this time much faster and brighter. The music started as well, louder and unmistakably the Bee Gees' "Stayin' Alive." Then the ball cracked open, in two clean pieces like a plastic Easter egg.

Inside there were two small Asian men. They were wearing hot pink short-shorts and black mesh wife-beaters. They were dancing and singing the song. Where the instrumental backup was coming from was a mystery.

They stopped singing and dancing and the music ceased as well. They stood up straight and spoke in unison, "Travelers, it is time for the foretold battle. You've been expected and we've been waiting. We know your journey has been long and difficult but it is time for it to come to an end."

Benny, Gary, and Janice looked at the small men in amazement.

"Ummm . . . who are you?" asked Benny.

"We are the avatars of the final battle. The rise of Shatzilla has been predicted since the beginning. He must be defeated. It is said that his rising will foretell the final battle. If he is not defeated, the whole world will lie in ruins. If he falls, there can be the rise of a new utopia."

"Whoa, what?" said Janice. "This is an awful lot to lay on us. What final battle?"

"Please," said the twins, "Shatzilla must be stopped before he leaves Los Angeles. If he's not, there may be no other opportunity to end his terror."

"What do you need us for?" said Benny. "It's not like we can do much against something that big."

"You must journey into the city, to the Black Cat Tavern

on sunset Boulevard. It is there that we can raise the one that can defeat Shatzilla."

"Defeat Shatzilla?" said Gary. "Are you talking about killing Shatner?"

"If that is what must be done."

"No, no way," said Gary. "I came all this way to save my friend. Not kill him."

"He is beyond saving at this point. The strange events taking place have morphed him into a different being. He is no longer the man you once knew. He is now a monster."

They were quiet for the moment while they considered the answer.

"So what do you think?" asked Benny looking at Gary.

"Please," said the twins. "If you truly value him, and the rest of the world, he must be stopped. There is no other option."

Gary sighed and nervously rubbed his forehead. He looked at Benny then Janice and then at the two little men starring up at him with pleading eyes.

"Gary," said Janice. "Remember *The City on the Edge of Forever*? Kirk didn't want to lose the woman he loved or hurt McCoy. But McCoy was on cordrazine and Edith Keeler had to die to stop the Nazis from winning the war. It was a hard and painful decision but it was the right one. This is your chance to be like Kirk."

Gary nodded his head, thinking.

"Fuck it," he said and looked at Benny, giving him a weak smile. "Let's stop William Shatner."

Benny nodded and turned to the twins. "So who are we going to get."

The twins bowed in unison and said, "The Takei."

23
REBIRTH OF TAKEI

"We should go on foot," said Benny. "The van is going to attract too much attention from Shatner."

Benny grabbed his satchel, the one that he used to carry Squishy around in. He felt a pang in his chest but quickly composed himself.

"Do you know how to get us there?" Benny asked the little men.

"Yes, we do," they said in unison.

He scooped them up and placed them in the bag. Their tiny heads poked out the top.

They pointed, "Down that way and take a left. It is not far but we must hurry."

They took off at a slight jog being careful to stick to the sides of buildings, they didn't want to get spotted by Shatzilla or anything else for that matter.

They could hear him though. They could hear his monster roars and hear the sounds of crunching metal and the occasional sound of someone screaming. They could even feel the stomp of his feet. They all hoped he wouldn't head in their direction.

After creeping down streets and alleys for fifteen minutes, the twins told them to stop.

"This is the place?" said Gary incredulously. They were in front of an unassuming bar with a sign above the front door that read BLACK CAT. He peered through the front windows and turned to look around. "There's no one here? I thought I was going to meet George Takei."

"Please place us on the ground," said the twins. "We must summon the Takei."

Benny carefully picked them out of his bag and placed them on the sidewalk in front of the bar.

"What's so special about this place?" asked Benny.

"Many years ago this was the site of an important event and the ground is still charged with the energy. But please, let us concentrate.

The twins held hands and shut their eyes. They looked like they were praying. Then, from some unknown source, disco music started to play. The two little men kept their eyes shut but unlocked their hands. They began to dance to the music.

"Where does that music keep coming from?" asked Janice as she looked around.

"So," said Gary. "I guess we just—"

His words stopped abruptly when a large piece of silver metal burst through his chest.

Just as quickly as it went through it was pulled out. Gary looked down at his chest, a dark red stain quickly spread across the gold fabric. He looked at Benny and Janice and tried to speak but blood poured from his mouth blocking the words. He fell to his knees and then fell face first. He was dead before his skull cracked against the ground.

Standing behind him, and brandishing a bloody bat'leth, was Koloth. His hair had all been burned away and his scalp was an open pus-streaming sore. Where his right eye should have been was black charred flesh. His costume was charred and torn and the exposed skin was red and peeling. What remained of his costume was black with soot. Somehow, his rubber ridges were still on his forehead.

He smiled at Benny and Janice. His pointed teeth made him look like a shark.

Janice was shocked and quietly said, "He killed Gary."

"You bastard," screamed Benny.

"And you're next," Koloth said. He then turned his attention to Janice and licked his teeth at her. "Maybe then I'll show her my bird of prey."

Then he saw the two dancing tiny Asian men on the sidewalk. "And what toys are you playing with?"

Koloth moved quickly, quicker than a man of that size and that badly burned should. He raised his foot to crush the two men.

"You fucking bastard," Benny screamed as he rushed forward. His vision was blurry from rage. First his cat died and now his best friend—all because of this fat fuck.

The street next to the sidewalk exploded upwards before Benny could reach Koloth, sending concrete and asphalt flying through the air. One of the hunks slammed into Koloth and sent him straight through the window of the bar, shattering the glass.

The ground shook more and Benny and Janice fell to their hands and knees.

"Behold," said the twins, "the Takei."

A giant human arm burst from the ground. Down the street, another arm shot up through the pavement. The hands gripped onto two buildings and the giant pulled himself out of the ground.

George Takei stood up and shook the debris off his body. He stood hundreds of feet tall, about the same size as William Shatner. He was wearing a very sensible designer suit cut to his exact measurements.

The giant Takei roared like an enraged gorilla. He looked around and dusted off his suit.

"Oh, myyy," he boomed.

"Oh, myyy," the twins repeated back. "All hail the Takei," the twins shouted and raised their arms.

Benny and Janice looked up in terror at the giant.

Takei beat his chest and roared at Shatzilla. The giant Shatner answered back and the *Boom Boom* of his steps rumbled the ground as he came to meet Takei. Takei moved forward to meet him.

Benny looked back at the bar searching for Koloth but didn't see him. He turned to the twins.

"So what happens now?" he asked.

"They fight," they said. "And one of them dies."

The two giants sized each other up in silence.

Shatner glared, "So . . . Mr. Sulu . . . we . . . meet again."

"Bill," Takei sighed, "for the last time, it's George."

"Have . . . at you," said Shatner and he charged Takei.

24
KAIJU SHATNER SHOWDOWN

Takei rushed forward, knocking over buildings with each step. Shatzilla moved forward to meet him.

"You know, Bill, you haven't aged well," said Takei

He pulled back his right arm and punched Shatner right in the jaw. The smack sounded like a bomb going off. Shatner's head flew back and Takei hit him in the gut with his left fist and then hit him again and again.

"The kids are all about me these days."

Shatner snorted and rubbed his jaw. "You're . . . just a fad . . . a . . . flavor of the week."

He darted forward and grabbed Takei's hair with both hands. He head-butted him three times and Takei's nose started to flow blood, dripping bucketfuls to the street below.

"They'll forget . . . about you . . . after . . . the next YouTube dance meme."

Takei jabbed up and hit Shatner right in the gut, knocking the air out of him.

"It's nice to see you at least lost the girdle, Bill. If only we could do something about your hair."

***

Benny and Janice got back to their feet and the two titans battled above them.

The two little men had their heads bowed with their eyes closed. They were holding hands and chanting, "Takei, Takei, Takei."

Benny turned and headed to the bar.

"Where are you going?" yelled Janice.

"After that fat fuck. I'm going to make sure he's dead."

"Oh, I hate to disappoint you."

They turned to see Koloth climbing out of the broken window to the bar. He was still gripping the bat'leth. He stepped onto the sidewalk and it took him great effort to stand up straight.

Benny screamed and charged at Koloth. The fat man had been beaten and burned but he was still surprisingly agile. He side-stepped and hit Benny in the back of the head with the dull side of the bat'leth.

Benny saw stars and staggered, surprised at the blow.

"Fuck me?" said Koloth as he hit Benny again with the dull side in the stomach. Benny dropped to his knees and gasped for air.

Koloth kicked him in the face, snapping his head back and sending blood and spit through the air.

"Fuck me? No, fuck you, you fucking fuck fuckers," he said and kicked Benny again. There was a loud crack as something broke. "I had everything. I was living like a king. Drugs, women, whatever I wanted." He coughed and spit a glob of blood and phlegm onto Benny. "And you took it all away. You and your goddamn cat."

Janice ran to attack Koloth from behind, but he spun and slammed the bat'leth into her side knocking her to the ground.

She tried getting up but Koloth was on top of her. He grabbed her hair and pulled her face back. He hit her quick and hard three times. Her eyes rolled around and blood poured from her torn open lip.

"Oh baby, I'll be with you soon enough." He looked back at Benny who was rolling on the ground. "I just gotta go finish with him." Koloth looked Janice in the eyes and smiled.

He's crazy, she thought.

He leaned in close to her and she tried to pull back but he was too strong. He stuck out his tongue and licked at the blood running down her chin.

She snapped her teeth forward trying to catch his tongue but missed.

"Feisty," he said and then back-handed her hard. She fell back to the ground.

Koloth stood up and walked over to Benny. Benny looked up at him with hate and tried to get to his feet. Koloth kicked him again in the side sending him rolling over.

"You're really not giving up are you?" said Koloth and smirked.

"Fuck . . . you," said Benny. "I'm . . . I'm still going to kill you."

"Awwww . . . are you mad that your widdle pussy cat is dead? Or was it killing your pathetic excuse for a best friend?" Koloth's smile grew even wider. "Or is it because I'm going to rape the shit out of that bitch?" He grabbed at his crotch, "I bet she ain't never taken it up the ass before. I'm going to tear her up."

Benny got up on his knees but Koloth hit him across the face again, knocking him over.

"How about I don't kill you? I could just break your arms and legs and make you watch."

Benny moaned.

"Ah, yeah. I can tell, you'd like that."

He raised the weapon over his head and let out a war cry that would make any Klingon proud.

And then the giant William Shatner stepped on him.

The battle between William Shatner and George Takei was still raging and Takei had gotten in another blow. Shatner staggered back and on the last step, as he regained balance, his left foot came down right on top of Koloth, missing Benny, Janice, and the twins by feet.

Shatner lifted his foot and rushed back into battle. All that was left of Koloth was a mashed-up mess of flesh, blood, and fabric smearing the street. Amongst the runny, chunky goo was Koloth's hand, still gripping the bat'leth.

***

Shatzilla grabbed Takei with both hands around his head and head-butted him again. He let him go, punched him in the face again, grabbed his head once more and pulled him close.

"They . . . forgot about you . . . for decades . . . and they'll . . . forget again."

163

Takei struggled but Shatner was just too strong. He got Takei's right ear right by his mouth, jutted forward, and bit it clean off. Shatner spit it out and the ear flew through the air landing several blocks away, crushing an SUV.

Takei screamed and Shatner hit him in the nose, the sound of it breaking was like a thunderclap. Takei fell to the ground.

"Do . . . you . . . really think you're . . . anything . . . compared to me?"

Takei laughed through the blood, "Bill, we both know you're a has been. You even named your album that. What's the next one going to be called? Desperately Struggling for Relevance?"

Shatner roared and rushed him. Takei shot out one of his legs and nailed Shatner right in the balls.

"Ugh," Shatner grunted and bowed over.

Takei leapt to his feet and grabbed at Shatner.

"Not . . . today," said Shatner and tossed Takei off, he was just so much bigger than him. He hit Takei in the back of the head and he fell to the ground again.

Shatzilla climbed on top and slammed his fist into Takei's face again and again.

***

The twins abruptly stopped chanting. They looked up in terror.

"Takei is failing." They turned and looked at Benny and Janice who were struggling to their feet. "He will lose without help."

Benny looked at them and then at Shatner pummeling Takei and then back to them. "What the fuck could we do?"

Janice narrowed her eyes at the two giants. "I know."

She ran to the mess that used to be Koloth and picked up the bat'leth. Koloth's hands still held strong. She ripped them off, breaking several of the fingers in the process.

With a loud cry she ran to the giants with the bat'leth raised high above her head. It took two blocks before she reached their feet. Takei's legs were stretched out straight, jerking with each blow that Shatner delivered.

Shatner was facing away from her, the backs of his legs and loafers toward her. The ankle socks he had on were pushed down low and his bare skin was visible.

She reached the giants and dodged their battle, looking for the right opportunity to strike. Shatzilla sat up and locked his fists together high above his head to deliver a punishing blow.

This was her chance. Janice ran forward and swung the bat'leth as hard as she could at the back of his right foot.

The blade passed through the flesh easily and then hit the thick rope that was his Achilles' tendon. Janice gripped the bat'leth harder and jerked it, slicing through the sinew. Blood poured down on her and the thick white tendon jutted out of his leg.

His leg thrashed back, hitting her, and sent her flying two blocks through the air right past Benny and crashing through one of the as yet undamaged windows of the Black Cat Tavern

***

Shatzilla fell to the ground, gripping his right ankle and howling in pain.

Takei got to his feet and looked down at Shatner, "oh Bill, you don't look so good."

Shatner grimaced through the pain. "Fuck . . . you Sulu . . . . I always . . . got . . . more groupies."

Takei smirked. "No, you didn't."

He raised his foot and slammed the black dress shoe down into Shatner's face, breaking his nose and squirting blood across the street and pavement. The force shook the ground and shattered nearby windows.

Shatner rolled on his side and tried to raise his arms in defense but Takei was quicker as he stomped his foot down again, smashing his lower jaw. Teeth the size of stadium seats clattered into the street.

Takei brought his foot down again and kept kicking and

stomping on Shatzilla's head as the giant weakly tried to fend off his attacker.

Takei finally stopped and moved back from his opponent. Shatner's broken jaw hung open, blood oozing up and over his hanging tongue. Blood poured from his nose and from his left eye socket. His right eye had popped out of his head and dangled down across his face. The face that millions knew and adored had been broken and bruised in so many places that it was near unrecognizable. Shatner wheezed for air and garbled from his ruined mouth.

Takei moved around him and sat down on the ground right above him. He braced his feet on Shatner's shoulders and grabbed his head beneath the neck. Shatzilla reached up and tried to pull away Takei's hands but there was no strength left in his body.

Takei pushed forward with his feet and pulled back with his hands.

Then there were sounds like redwood trees splitting and falling over.

Shatner stopped trying to fight back and started to convulse. His neck got longer and longer, too long. Then the flesh started to tear.

It happened suddenly. Shatner's head tore free from his body and Takei fell onto his back. He looked down and smiled and the body poured blood like an open sewer drain from the stump.

Takei rose to his feet and held up the severed head of William Shatner high above L.A. The eyes dangled down and the neck dripped blood and mutilated flesh.

"OHHHH MMYYYYYY!" he roared and then tossed the head away.

***

"The Takei has won," said the twins with beaming smiles but Benny did not hear them.

He was inside the restaurant, pulling out Janice's limp body from beneath broken tables and chairs. Her eyes were closed and she was unresponsive. But she was still breathing.

Benny carried her outside to get her into the light and lay her down on ground that wasn't covered with broken glass and wood. He laid her out flat on the concrete.

"Please, please, please," he repeated.

And then she started to cough. After a few moments, she regained composure and opened her eyes.

"Did it work?" she asked.

"Yes, yes it did," said Benny, tears in his eyes. He kissed her. He wasn't thinking, he was just so happy she was still alive.

It was brief—it lasted just a moment before he realized what he was doing and pulled back embarrassed.

Janice smiled. "Can you help me to my feet?"

He did and they both turned to look at the giant George Takei who was walking to them.

He reached the other side of the street and looked down at them, smiling like an old, gay grandfather.

"My new friends, thank you," said Takei

"Without you Shatzilla would rule the world. We can not express our gratitude," chimed in the twins.

"Ummm . . . you're welcome," said Benny.

The twins bowed. "It is time for us to go. This is not the only pressing matter that the Takei needs to address."

The giant George Takei leaned over and put his hand on the ground, palm up. The twins climbed up the huge fingers and they stood in the center of the palm.

"I don't believe this will be the last time we meet," said the Takei. His face started to swell with bruises.

The twins waved goodbye to Benny and Janice. "Thank you again. And good luck. A brave new world is possible."

Takei's hand raised them high into the air and Benny and Janice waved goodbye.

Takei turned away from them and began to walk in the direction of the ocean, each step shaking the ground.

Benny and Janice watched them until they crested over the horizon and were out of sight.

"Oh myyy!" he bellowed one last time in the distance, and then they were gone.

25
IMAGINE THIS IS THE LAST SCENE OF A MOVIE NARRATED BY MORGAN FREEMAN FOR MAXIMUM IMPACT

And so, for the second time in their lives, Benny and Janice headed out on the road, unsure of what their final destination would bring.

They were exhausted, emotionally and physically. They had traveled across the entire country and lost close friends. And now they were bruised and bloodied and the very thing they had come to save, they destroyed.

Their hearts were heavy but they had not given up and were not going to just give up.

They moved silently through the streets, careful not to attract the attention of the Zombie Borg. But there were others.

They were not the only survivors. There were others hidden in basements and shelters of those fortunate still-standing buildings. They saw the fall of Shatner and these two saviors leaving the city.

They came out of their hiding places and followed behind Benny and Janice. They kept their distance from the two but made sure to follow their example of not drawing the Zombie Borg's attention.

As they traveled, more and more people came out of their hiding places and joined the exodus from the city.

Benny and Janice kept moving forward. They knew there were people following them but they didn't say anything or look back. They continued through rubble and wreckage until finally they came to a road leading up a mountain and out of Los Angeles.

They walked and stopped at an overlook point where they could see the whole city. William Shatner's massive corpse was sprawled out across many blocks and they could see that the Zombie Borg were already moving around it, shoving wires into the recently dead flesh. Shatner's head had landed almost a mile away from the body and was upside down, the bloody stump pointing straight into the air and an eye dangling down his forehead.

The Zombie Borg increased in number, filling the streets. The walking corpses moved through the city as their infection spread.

The surviving people left the city and followed the road to where Benny and Janice overlooked them. They could see the faces of some of those closest. They were ragged and weary but their eyes shone with light. They had something they hadn't had since the world went crazy—hope.

"So," said Janice, finally breaking the silence. "What do we do now?"

"Those tiny guys said if Shatner was stopped there could be a utopia."

"And how does that work?"

Benny smiled. "I have no idea."

He reached over and took her hand in his. Janice smiled too.

They held hands and walked away from the city. Los Angeles burned but they did not look back again. They moved forward, and led their followers into a brave new world.

JEFF BURK ⟨⟨⟩⟩⟨⟩ ⟨⟨⟩⟨⟩ ⟨⟨⟨⟨⟨⟨⟨⟨ ⟨⟨ ⟨⟨⟨⟩ ⟨⟩ ⟨⟨⟨⟨⟨⟨⟨⟨ *Shatnerquake, Super Giant Monster Time,* ⟨⟨ *Cripple Wolf.* ⟨⟨⟨⟩ ⟨⟩ ⟨⟨⟨ ⟨⟨ Deadite Press ⟨⟨ ⟨⟨⟨ ⟨⟨⟩ The Magazine of Bizarro Fiction. ⟨⟨⟨⟩ ⟨⟨⟩ ⟨⟨⟨⟨⟨ ⟨⟨⟨⟨⟨ ⟨⟨⟨⟨⟨⟨⟨⟨ ⟨⟨⟩ ⟨⟨⟩ ⟨⟨ ⟨⟨⟨⟩:

www.JeffBurk.wordpress.com
www.facebook.com/LiteraryStrange
www.twitter.com/Jeff_Burk

Bizarro Books

CATALOG   SPRING 2012

ERASERHEAD PRESS

Your major resource for the bizarro fiction genre:

WWW.BIZARROCENTRAL.COM

Introduce yourselves to the bizarro fiction genre and all of its authors with the Bizarro Starter Kit series. Each volume features short novels and short stories by ten of the leading bizarro authors, designed to give you a perfect sampling of the genre for only $10.

BB-0X1
"The Bizarro Starter Kit" (Orange)

Featuring D. Harlan Wilson, Carlton Mellick III, Jeremy Robert Johnson, Kevin L Donihe, Gina Ranalli, Andre Duza, Vincent W. Sakowski, Steve Beard, John Edward Lawson, and Bruce Taylor. **236 pages $10**

BB-0X2
"The Bizarro Starter Kit" (Blue)

Featuring Ray Fracalossy, Jeremy C. Shipp, Jordan Krall, Mykle Hansen, Andersen Prunty, Eckhard Gerdes, Bradley Sands, Steve Aylett, Christian TeBordo, and Tony Rauch. **244 pages $10**

BB-0X2
"The Bizarro Starter Kit" (Purple)

Featuring Russell Edson, Athena Villaverde, David Agranoff, Matthew Revert, Andrew Goldfarb, Jeff Burk, Garrett Cook, Kris Saknussemm, Cody Goodfellow, and Cameron Pierce **264 pages $10**

BB-001 **"The Kafka Effekt" D. Harlan Wilson** — A collection of forty-four irreal short stories loosely written in the vein of Franz Kafka, with more than a pinch of William S. Burroughs sprinkled on top. **211 pages $14**

BB-002 **"Satan Burger" Carlton Mellick III** — The cult novel that put Carlton Mellick III on the map ... Six punks get jobs at a fast food restaurant owned by the devil in a city violently overpopulated by surreal alien cultures. **236 pages $14**

BB-003 **"Some Things Are Better Left Unplugged" Vincent Sakwoski** — Join The Man and his Nemesis, the obese tabby, for a nightmare roller coaster ride into this postmodern fantasy. **152 pages $10**

BB-004 **"Shall We Gather At the Garden?" Kevin L Donihe** — Donihe's Debut novel. Midgets take over the world, The Church of Lionel Richie vs. The Church of the Byrds, plant porn and more! **244 pages $14**

BB-005 **"Razor Wire Pubic Hair" Carlton Mellick III** — A genderless humandildo is purchased by a razor dominatrix and brought into her nightmarish world of bizarre sex and mutilation. **176 pages $11**

BB-006 **"Stranger on the Loose" D. Harlan Wilson** — The fiction of Wilson's 2nd collection is planted in the soil of normalcy, but what grows out of that soil is a dark, witty, otherworldly jungle... **228 pages $14**

BB-007 **"The Baby Jesus Butt Plug" Carlton Mellick III** — Using clones of the Baby Jesus for anal sex will be the hip sex fetish of the future. **92 pages $10**

BB-008 **"Fishyfleshed" Carlton Mellick III** — The world of the past is an illogical flatland lacking in dimension and color, a sick-scape of crispy squid people wandering the desert for no apparent reason. **260 pages $14**

BB-009 "Dead Bitch Army" Andre Duza — Step into a world filled with racist teenagers, cannibals, 100 warped Uncle Sams, automobiles with razor-sharp teeth, living graffiti, and a pissed-off zombie bitch out for revenge. **344 pages $16**

BB-010 "The Menstruating Mall" Carlton Mellick III — "The Breakfast Club meets Chopping Mall as directed by David Lynch." - Brian Keene **212 pages $12**

BB-011 "Angel Dust Apocalypse" Jeremy Robert Johnson — Meth-heads, man-made monsters, and murderous Neo-Nazis. "Seriously amazing short stories..." - Chuck Palahniuk, author of Fight Club **184 pages $11**

BB-012 "Ocean of Lard" Kevin L Donihe / Carlton Mellick III — A parody of those old Choose Your Own Adventure kid's books about some very odd pirates sailing on a sea made of animal fat. **176 pages $12**

BB-015 "Foop!" Chris Genoa — Strange happenings are going on at Dactyl, Inc, the world's first and only time travel tourism company.
"A surreal pie in the face!" - Christopher Moore **300 pages $14**

BB-020 "Punk Land" Carlton Mellick III — In the punk version of Heaven, the anarchist utopia is threatened by corporate fascism and only Goblin, Mortician's sperm, and a blue-mohawked female assassin named Shark Girl can stop them. **284 pages $15**

BB-027 "Siren Promised" Jeremy Robert Johnson & Alan M Clark — Nominated for the Bram Stoker Award. A potent mix of bad drugs, bad dreams, brutal bad guys, and surreal/incredible art by Alan M. Clark. **190 pages $13**

BB-031 "Sea of the Patchwork Cats" Carlton Mellick III — A quiet dreamlike tale set in the ashes of the human race. For Mellick enthusiasts who also adore The Twilight Zone. **112 pages $10**

BB-032 "Extinction Journals" Jeremy Robert Johnson — An uncanny voyage across a newly nuclear America where one man must confront the problems associated with loneliness, insane dieties, radiation, love, and an ever-evolving cockroach suit with a mind of its own. **104 pages $10**

BB-037 "The Haunted Vagina" Carlton Mellick III — It's difficult to love a woman whose vagina is a gateway to the world of the dead. **132 pages $10**

BB-043 "War Slut" Carlton Mellick III — Part "1984," part "Waiting for Godot," and part action horror video game adaptation of John Carpenter's "The Thing." **116 pages $10**

BB-047 "Sausagey Santa" Carlton Mellick III — A bizarro Christmas tale featuring Santa as a piratey mutant with a body made of sausages. 124 pages $10

BB-048 "Misadventures in a Thumbnail Universe" Vincent Sakowski — Dive deep into the surreal and satirical realms of neo-classical Blender Fiction, filled with television shoes and flesh-filled skies. **120 pages $10**

BB-053 "Ballad of a Slow Poisoner" Andrew Goldfarb — Millford Mutterwurst sat down on a Tuesday to take his afternoon tea, and made the unpleasant discovery that his elbows were becoming flatter. **128 pages $10**

BB-055 "Help! A Bear is Eating Me" Mykle Hansen — The bizarro, heartwarming, magical tale of poor planning, hubris and severe blood loss... **150 pages $11**

BB-056 "Piecemeal June" Jordan Krall — A man falls in love with a living sex doll, but with love comes danger when her creator comes after her with crab-squid assassins. **90 pages $9**

BB-058 **"The Overwhelming Urge" Andersen Prunty** — A collection of bizarro tales by Andersen Prunty. **150 pages $11**

BB-059 **"Adolf in Wonderland" Carlton Mellick III** — A dreamlike adventure that takes a young descendant of Adolf Hitler's design and sends him down the rabbit hole into a world of imperfection and disorder. **180 pages $11**

BB-061 **"Ultra Fuckers" Carlton Mellick III** — Absurdist suburban horror about a couple who enter an upper middle class gated community but can't find their way out. **108 pages $9**

BB-062 **"House of Houses" Kevin L. Donihe** — An odd man wants to marry his house. Unfortunately, all of the houses in the world collapse at the same time in the Great House Holocaust. Now he must travel to House Heaven to find his departed fiancee. **172 pages $11**

BB-064 **"Squid Pulp Blues" Jordan Krall** — In these three bizarro-noir novellas, the reader is thrown into a world of murderers, drugs made from squid parts, deformed gun-toting veterans, and a mischievous apocalyptic donkey. **204 pages $12**

BB-065 **"Jack and Mr. Grin" Andersen Prunty** — "When Mr. Grin calls you can hear a smile in his voice. Not a warm and friendly smile, but the kind that seizes your spine in fear. You don't need to pay your phone bill to hear it. That smile is in every line of Prunty's prose." - Tom Bradley. **208 pages $12**

BB-066 **"Cybernetrix" Carlton Mellick III** — What would you do if your normal everyday world was slowly mutating into the video game world from Tron? **212 pages $12**

BB-072 **"Zerostrata" Andersen Prunty** — Hansel Nothing lives in a tree house, suffers from memory loss, has a very eccentric family, and falls in love with a woman who runs naked through the woods every night. **144 pages $11**

BB-073 "The Egg Man" Carlton Mellick III — It is a world where humans reproduce like insects. Children are the property of corporations, and having an enormous ten-foot brain implanted into your skull is a grotesque sexual fetish. Mellick's industrial urban dystopia is one of his darkest and grittiest to date. **184 pages $11**

BB-074 "Shark Hunting in Paradise Garden" Cameron Pierce — A group of strange humanoid religious fanatics travel back in time to the Garden of Eden to discover it is invested with hundreds of giant flying maneating sharks. **150 pages $10**

BB-075 "Apeshit" Carlton Mellick III - Friday the 13th meets Visitor Q. Six hipster teens go to a cabin in the woods inhabited by a deformed killer. An incredibly fucked-up parody of B-horror movies with a bizarro slant. **192 pages $12**

BB-076 "Fuckers of Everything on the Crazy Shitting Planet of the Vomit At smosphere" Mykle Hansen - Three bizarro satires. Monster Cocks, Journey to the Center of Agnes Cuddlebottom, and Crazy Shitting Planet. **228 pages $12**

BB-077 "The Kissing Bug" Daniel Scott Buck — In the tradition of Roald Dahl, Tim Burton, and Edward Gorey, comes this bizarro anti-war children's story about a bohemian conenose kissing bug who falls in love with a human woman. **116 pages $10**

BB-078 "MachoPoni" Lotus Rose — It's My Little Pony... *Bizarro* style! A long time ago Poniworld was split in two. On one side of the Jagged Line is the Pastel Kingdom, a magical land of music, parties, and positivity. On the other side of the Jagged Line is Dark Kingdom inhabited by an army of undead ponies. **148 pages $11**

BB-079 "The Faggiest Vampire" Carlton Mellick III — A Roald Dahl-esque children's story about two faggy vampires who partake in a mustache competition to find out which one is truly the faggiest. **104 pages $10**

BB-080 "Sky Tongues" Gina Ranalli — The autobiography of Sky Tongues, the biracial hermaphrodite actress with tongues for fingers. Follow her strange life story as she rises from freak to fame. **204 pages $12**

BB-081 "Washer Mouth" Kevin L. Donihe - A washing machine becomes human and pursues his dream of meeting his favorite soap opera star. **244 pages $11**

BB-082 "Shatnerquake" Jeff Burk - All of the characters ever played by William Shatner are suddenly sucked into our world. Their mission: hunt down and destroy the real William Shatner. **100 pages $10**

BB-083 "The Cannibals of Candyland" Carlton Mellick III - There exists a race of cannibals that are made of candy. They live in an underground world made out of candy. One man has dedicated his life to killing them all. **170 pages $11**

BB-084 "Slub Glub in the Weird World of the Weeping Willows" Andrew Goldfarb - The charming tale of a blue glob named Slub Glub who helps the weeping willows whose tears are flooding the earth. There are also hyenas, ghosts, and a voodoo priest **100 pages $10**

BB-085 "Super Fetus" Adam Pepper - Try to abort this fetus and he'll kick your ass! **104 pages $10**

BB-086 "Fistful of Feet" Jordan Krall - A bizarro tribute to spaghetti westerns, featuring Cthulhu-worshipping Indians, a woman with four feet, a crazed gunman who is obsessed with sucking on candy, Syphilis-ridden mutants, sexually transmitted tattoos, and a house devoted to the freakiest fetishes. **228 pages $12**

BB-087 "Ass Goblins of Auschwitz" Cameron Pierce - It's Monty Python meets Nazi exploitation in a surreal nightmare as can only be imagined by Bizarro author Cameron Pierce. **104 pages $10**

BB-088 "Silent Weapons for Quiet Wars" Cody Goodfellow - "This is high-end psychological surrealist horror meets bottom-feeding low-life crime in a techno-thrilling science fiction world full of Lovecraft and magic..." -John Skipp **212 pages $12**

BB-089 "Warrior Wolf Women of the Wasteland" Carlton Mellick III

— Road Warrior Werewolves versus McDonaldland Mutants...post-apocalyptic fiction has never been quite like this. **316 pages $13**

BB-091 "Super Giant Monster Time" Jeff Burk

— A tribute to choose your own adventures and Godzilla movies. Will you escape the giant monsters that are rampaging the fuck out of your city and shit? Or will you join the mob of alien-controlled punk rockers causing chaos in the streets? What happens next depends on you. **188 pages $12**

BB-092 "Perfect Union" Cody Goodfellow

— "Cronenberg's THE FLY on a grand scale: human/insect gene-spliced body horror, where the human hive politics are as shocking as the gore." -John Skipp. **272 pages $13**

BB-093 "Sunset with a Beard" Carlton Mellick III

— 14 stories of surreal science fiction. **200 pages $12**

BB-094 "My Fake War" Andersen Prunty

— The absurd tale of an unlikely soldier forced to fight a war that, quite possibly, does not exist. It's Rambo meets Waiting for Godot in this subversive satire of American values and the scope of the human imagination. **128 pages $11**

BB-095 "Lost in Cat Brain Land" Cameron Pierce

— Sad stories from a surreal world. A fascist mustache, the ghost of Franz Kafka, a desert inside a dead cat. Primordial entities mourn the death of their child. The desperate serve tea to mysterious creatures. A hopeless romantic falls in love with a pterodactyl. And much more. **152 pages $11**

BB-096 "The Kobold Wizard's Dildo of Enlightenment +2" Carlton Mellick III

— A Dungeons and Dragons parody about a group of people who learn they are only made up characters in an AD&D campaign and must find a way to resist their nerdy teenaged players and retarded dungeon master in order to survive. 232 **pages $12**

BB-098 "A Hundred Horrible Sorrows of Ogner Stump" Andrew Goldfarb

— Goldfarb's acclaimed comic series. A magical and weird journey into the horrors of everyday life. **164 pages $11**

BB-099 **"Pickled Apocalypse of Pancake Island" Cameron Pierce**—A demented fairy tale about a pickle, a pancake, and the apocalypse. **102 pages $8**

BB-100 **"Slag Attack" Andersen Prunty**— Slag Attack features four visceral, noir stories about the living, crawling apocalypse.A slag is what survivors are calling the slug-like maggots raining from the sky, burrowing inside people, and hollowing out their flesh and their sanity. **148 pages $11**

BB-101 **"Slaughterhouse High" Robert Devereaux**—A place where schools are built with secret passageways, rebellious teens get zippers installed in their mouths and genitals, and once a year, on that special night, one couple is slaughtered and the bits of their bodies are kept as souvenirs. **304 pages $13**

BB-102 **"The Emerald Burrito of Oz" John Skipp & Marc Levinthal** —OZ IS REAL! Magic is real! The gate is really in Kansas! And America is finally allowing Earth tourists to visit this weird-ass, mysterious land. But when Gene of Los Angeles heads off for summer vacation in the Emerald City, little does he know that a war is brewing...a war that could destroy both worlds. **280 pages $13**

BB-103 **"The Vegan Revolution... with Zombies" David Agranoff** — When there's no more meat in hell, the vegans will walk the earth. **160 pages $11**

BB-104 **"The Flappy Parts" Kevin L Donihe**—Poems about bunnies, LSD, and police abuse. You know, things that matter. 132 **pages $11**

BB-105 **"Sorry I Ruined Your Orgy" Bradley Sands**—Bizarro humorist Bradley Sands returns with one of the strangest, most hilarious collections of the year. **130 pages $11**

BB-106 **"Mr. Magic Realism" Bruce Taylor**—Like Golden Age science fiction comics written by Freud, *Mr. Magic Realism* is a strange, insightful adventure that spans the furthest reaches of the galaxy, exploring the hidden caverns in the hearts and minds of men, women, aliens, and biomechanical cats. **152 pages $11**

BB-107 "Zombies and Shit" Carlton Mellick III—"Battle Royale" meets "Return of the Living Dead." Mellick's bizarro tribute to the zombie genre. **308 pages $13**

BB-108 "The Cannibal's Guide to Ethical Living" Mykle Hansen— Over a five star French meal of fine wine, organic vegetables and human flesh, a lunatic delivers a witty, chilling, disturbingly sane argument in favor of eating the rich.. **184 pages $11**

BB-109 "Starfish Girl" Athena Villaverde—In a post-apocalyptic underwater dome society, a girl with a starfish growing from her head and an assassin with sea anenome hair are on the run from a gang of mutant fish men. **160 pages $11**

BB-110 "Lick Your Neighbor" Chris Genoa—Mutant ninjas, a talking whale, kung fu masters, maniacal pilgrims, and an alcoholic clown populate Chris Genoa's surreal, darkly comical and unnerving reimagining of the first Thanksgiving. **303 pages $13**

BB-111 "Night of the Assholes" Kevin L. Donihe—A plague of assholes is infecting the countryside. Normal everyday people are transforming into jerks, snobs, dicks, and douchebags. And they all have only one purpose: to make your life a living hell.. **192 pages $11**

BB-112 "Jimmy Plush, Teddy Bear Detective" Garrett Cook—Hardboiled cases of a private detective trapped within a teddy bear body. **180 pages $11**

BB-113 "The Deadheart Shelters" Forrest Armstrong—The hip hop lovechild of William Burroughs and Dali... **144 pages $11**

BB-114 "Eyeballs Growing All Over Me... Again" Tony Raugh— Absurd, surreal, playful, dream-like, whimsical, and a lot of fun to read. **144 pages $11**

BB-115 **"Whargoul" Dave Brockie** — From the killing grounds of Stalingrad to the death camps of the holocaust. From torture chambers in Iraq to race riots in the United States, the Whargoul was there, killing and raping. **244 pages $12**

BB-116 **"By the Time We Leave Here, We'll Be Friends" J. David Osborne** — A David Lynchian nightmare set in a Russian gulag, where its prisoners, guards, traitors, soldiers, lovers, and demons fight for survival and their own rapidly deteriorating humanity. **168 pages $11**

BB-117 **"Christmas on Crack" edited by Carlton Mellick III** — Perverted Christmas Tales for the whole family! . . . as long as every member of your family is over the age of 18. **168 pages $11**

BB-118 **"Crab Town" Carlton Mellick III** — Radiation fetishists, balloon people, mutant crabs, sail-bike road warriors, and a love affair between a woman and an H-Bomb. This is one mean asshole of a city. Welcome to Crab Town. **100 pages $8**

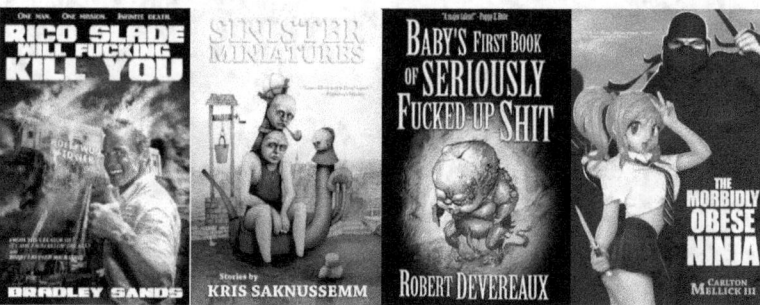

BB-119 **"Rico Slade Will Fucking Kill You" Bradley Sands** — Rico Slade is an action hero. Rico Slade can rip out a throat with his bare hands. Rico Slade's favorite food is the honey-roasted peanut. Rico Slade will fucking kill everyone. A novel. **122 pages $8**

BB-120 **"Sinister Miniatures" Kris Saknussemm** — The definitive collection of short fiction by Kris Saknussemm, confirming that he is one of the best, most daring writers of the weird to emerge in the twenty-first century. **180 pages $11**

BB-121 **"Baby's First Book of Seriously Fucked up Shit" Robert Devereaux** — Ten stories of the strange, the gross, and the just plain fucked up from one of the most original voices in horror. **176 pages $11**

BB-122 **"The Morbidly Obese Ninja" Carlton Mellick III** — These days, if you want to run a successful company . . . you're going to need a lot of ninjas. **92 pages $8**

BB-123 **"Abortion Arcade" Cameron Pierce** — An intoxicating blend of body horror and midnight movie madness, reminiscent of early David Lynch and the splatterpunks at their most sublime. **172 pages $11**

BB-124 **"Black Hole Blues" Patrick Wensink** — A hilarious double helix of country music and physics. **196 pages $11**

BB-125 **"Barbarian Beast Bitches of the Badlands" Carlton Mellick III** — Three prequels and sequels to *Warrior Wolf Women of the Wasteland.* **284 pages $13**

BB-126 **"The Traveling Dildo Salesman" Kevin L. Donihe** — A nightmare comedy about destiny, faith, and sex toys. Also featuring Donihe's most lurid and infamous short stories: *Milky Agitation, Two-Way Santa, The Helen Mower, Living Room Zombies,* and *Revenge of the Living Masturbation Rag.* **108 pages $8**

BB-127 **"Metamorphosis Blues" Bruce Taylor** — Enter a land of love beasts, intergalactic cowboys, and rock 'n roll. A land where Sears Catalogs are doorways to insanity and men keep mysterious black boxes. Welcome to the monstrous mind of Mr. Magic Realism. **136 pages $11**

BB-128 **"The Driver's Guide to Hitting Pedestrians" Andersen Prunty** — A pocket guide to the twenty-three most painful things in life, written by the most well-adjusted man in the universe. **108 pages $8**

BB-129 **"Island of the Super People" Kevin Shamel** — Four students and their anthropology professor journey to a remote island to study its indigenous population. But this is no ordinary native culture. They're super heroes and villains with flesh costumes and out-landish abilities like self-detonation, musical eyelashes, and microwave hands. **194 pages $11**

BB-130 **"Fantastic Orgy" Carlton Mellick III** — Shark Sex, mutant cats, and strange sexually transmitted diseases. Featuring the stories: *Candy-coated, Ear Cat, Fantastic Orgy, City Hobgoblins,* and *Porno in August.* **136 pages $9**

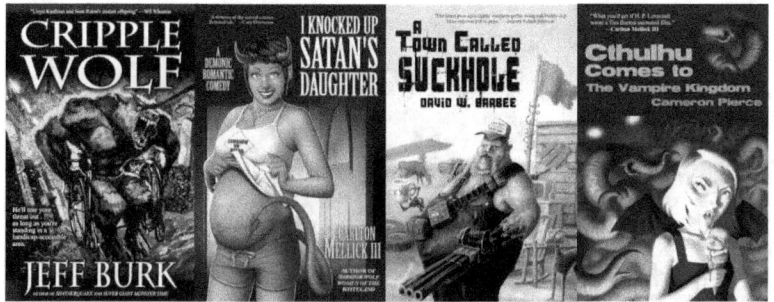

BB-131 **"Cripple Wolf" Jeff Burk** — Part man. Part wolf. 100% crippled. Also including *Punk Rock Nursing Home, Adrift with Space Badgers, Cook for Your Life, Just Another Day in the Park, Frosty and the Full Monty*, and *House of Cats*. **152 pages $10**

BB-132 **"I Knocked Up Satan's Daughter" Carlton Mellick III** — An adorable, violent, fantastical love story. A romantic comedy for the bizarro fiction reader. **152 pages $10**

BB-133 **"A Town Called Suckhole" David W. Barbee** — Far into the future, in the nuclear bowels of post-apocalyptic Dixie, there is a town. A town of derelict mobile homes, ancient junk, and mutant wildlife. A town of slack jawed rednecks who bask in the splendors of moonshine and mud boggin'. A town dedicated to the bloody and demented legacy of the Old South. A town called Suckhole. **144 pages $10**

BB-134 **"Cthulhu Comes to the Vampire Kingdom" Cameron Pierce** — What you'd get if H. P. Lovecraft wrote a Tim Burton animated film. **148 pages $11**

BB-135 **"I am Genghis Cum" Violet LeVoit** — From the savage Arctic tundra to post-partum mutations to your missing daughter's unmarked grave, join visionary madwoman Violet LeVoit in this non-stop eight-story onslaught of full-tilt Bizarro punk lit thrills. **124 pages $9**

BB-136 **"Haunt" Laura Lee Bahr** — A tripping-balls Los Angeles noir, where a mysterious dame drags you through a time-warping Bizarro hall of mirrors. **316 pages $13**

BB-137 **"Amazing Stories of the Flying Spaghetti Monster" edited by Cameron Pierce** — Like an all-spaghetti evening of Adult Swim, the Flying Spaghetti Monster will show you the many realms of His Noodly Appendage. Learn of those who worship him and the lives he touches in distant, mysterious ways. **228 pages $12**

BB-138 **"Wave of Mutilation" Douglas Lain** — A dream-pop exploration of modern architecture and the American identity, *Wave of Mutilation* is a Zen finger trap for the 21st century. **100 pages $8**

BB-139 **"Hooray for Death!" Mykle Hansen** — Famous Author Mykle Hansen draws unconventional humor from deaths tiny and large, and invites you to laugh while you can. **128 pages $10**

BB-140 **"Hypno-hog's Moonshine Monster Jamboree" Andrew Goldfarb** — Hicks, Hogs, Horror! Goldfarb is back with another strange illustrated tale of backwoods weirdness. **120 pages $9**

BB-141 **"Broken Piano For President" Patrick Wensink** — A comic masterpiece about the fast food industry, booze, and the necessity to choose happiness over work and security. **372 pages $15**

BB-142 **"Please Do Not Shoot Me in the Face" Bradley Sands** — A novel in three parts, *Please Do Not Shoot Me in the Face: A Novel*, is the story of one boy detective, the worst ninja in the world, and the great American fast food wars. It is a novel of loss, destruction, and--incredibly--genuine hope. **224 pages $12**

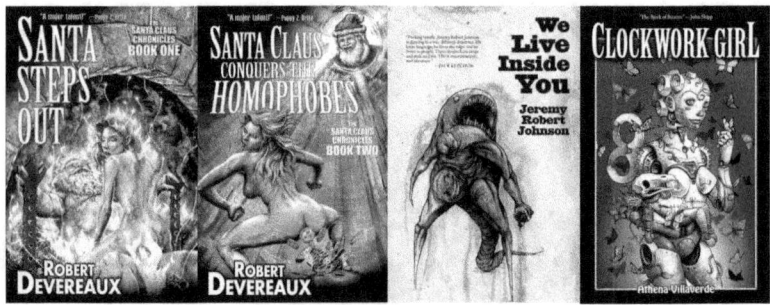

BB-143 **"Santa Steps Out" Robert Devereaux** — Sex, Death, and Santa Claus ... The ultimate erotic Christmas story is back. **294 pages $13**

BB-144 **"Santa Conquers the Homophobes" Robert Devereaux** — "I wish I could hope to ever attain one-thousandth the perversity of Robert Devereaux's toenail clippings." - Poppy Z. Brite **316 pages $13**

BB-145 **"We Live Inside You" Jeremy Robert Johnson** — "Jeremy Robert Johnson is dancing to a way different drummer. He loves language, he loves the edge, and he loves us people. These stories have range and style and wit. This is entertainment... and literature."- Jack Ketchum **188 pages $11**

BB-146 **"Clockwork Girl" Athena Villaverde** — Urban fairy tales for the weird girl in all of us. Like a combination of Francesca Lia Block, Charles de Lint, Kathe Koja, Tim Burton, and Hayao Miyazaki, her stories are cute, kinky, edgy, magical, provocative, and strange, full of poetic imagery and vicious sexuality. **160 pages $10**

BB-147 **"Armadillo Fists" Carlton Mellick III** — A weird-as-hell gangster story set in a world where people drive giant mechanical dinosaurs instead of cars. **168 pages $11**

BB-148 **"Gargoyle Girls of Spider Island" Cameron Pierce** — Four college seniors venture out into open waters for the tropical party weekend of a lifetime. Instead of a teenage sex fantasy, they find themselves in a nightmare of pirates, sharks, and sex-crazed monsters. **100 pages $8**

BB-149 **"The Handsome Squirm" by Carlton Mellick III** — Like Franz Kafka's *The Trial* meets an erotic body horror version of *The Blob.* **158 pages $11**

BB-150 **"Tentacle Death Trip" Jordan Krall** — It's *Death Race 2000* meets H. P. Lovecraft in bizarro author Jordan Krall's best and most suspenseful work to date. **224 pages $12**

BB-151 **"The Obese" Nick Antosca** — Like Alfred Hitchcock's *The Birds...* but with obese people. **108 pages $10**

BB-152 **"All-Monster Action!" Cody Goodfellow** — The world gave him a blank check and a demand: Create giant monsters to fight our wars. But Dr. Otaku was not satisfied with mere chaos and mass destruction.... **216 pages $12**

BB-153 **"Ugly Heaven" Carlton Mellick III** — Heaven is no longer a paradise. It was once a blissful utopia full of wonders far beyond human comprehension. But the afterlife is now in ruins. It has become an ugly, lonely wasteland populated by strange monstrous beasts, masturbating angels, and sad man-like beings wallowing in the remains of the once-great Kingdom of God. **106 pages $8**

BB-154 **"Space Walrus" Kevin L. Donihe** — Walter is supposed to go where no walrus has ever gone before, but all this astronaut walrus really wants is to take it easy on the intense training, escape the chimpanzee bullies, and win the love of his human trainer Dr. Stephanie. **160 pages $11**